Heart of
ALLEGIANCE

D1024560

Heart of
ALLEGIANCE

Jake & Luke Thoene

THOMAS NELSON PUBLISHERS
Nashville

Copyright © 1998 by Jake Thoene and Luke Thoene

Published in association with the literary agency of Alive Communications, 1465 Kelly Johnson Blvd., Suite #320, Colorado Springs, CO 80920

All rights reserved. Written permission must be secured from the publisher to use or reproduce any part of this book, except for brief quotations in critical reviews or articles.

Published in Nashville, Tennessee, by Thomas Nelson, Inc.

Library of Congress Cataloging-in-Publication Data

Thoene, Jake.
    Heart of allegiance : a novel / Jake Thoene and Luke Thoene.
        p.   cm. — (Portraits of destiny / Jake Thoene and Luke
    Thoene.)
    ISBN 0-7852-7145-7 (pbk.)
    I. Thoene, Luke. II. Title. III. Series: Thoene, Jake. Portraits of
    destiny.
    PS3570.H465H4   1998
    813'.54—DC21   97-36575
                                                                   CIP

Printed in the United States of America

1 2 3 4 5 6 7 QPK 04 03 02 01 00 99 98

To Marshall Hall,
educator and friend.

PROLOGUE

The howl of the wind drowned out the thin cries of the tiny babies.

The brig *Hermes* was only six miles off the French island of Ouessant when the weather turned foul. Her rigging whining in protest at the strain, the timbers of the two-masted merchantman groaned as if she were laboring to birth passengers and cargo into the tossing waves. She might easily have been in the mid-Atlantic for the fierceness of the gale.

Upon her departure from Oporto only two days before, Captain Jonathan Appiano had sniffed the dusty offshore breeze and predicted calm seas and light winds for the entire crossing to Dover. As the son and heir of the ship's owner, Bryce Sutton placed full confidence in his father's most senior captain. The month of October was generally accommodating for shipping up the channel toward England, even for an over-freighted ship like the *Hermes*. But that autumn of 1780, an unseasonably early storm alighted on the eastern reaches, and nothing remained but to ride it out. Appiano ordered the hatches battened and shortened sail to a pair of triple-reefed tops.

On the sailing manifest, listed beneath silks and Spanish perfumes, were two hundred weighty casks of port wine. These had a special reason for being aboard: fifty barrels were destined for a grand reception to follow the christenings of the newest Sutton heirs; the twin boys William and Charles. The three-month-old babies were squalling lustily in the captain's cabin.

Rain poured over the decks and jetted out the scuppers as though shot from cannons. Lightning bolts turned the planks and spars an eerie gray hue as they lanced into nearby swells. While the southwesterly blasted them, Appiano and his crew stood shivering at their posts, fighting for control of the ship. The tiller was manned by four brawny Jerseymen, but none of their efforts could prevent the brig from veering crazily. With each racing twenty-foot-high swell of the following sea, the *Hermes* was heaved up sternmost, then left to flounder backward down the reverse slope. From one moment to the next, she was either poised to dig her bowsprit into the depths or to be crushed from behind by a mass of water traveling faster than the ship could sail to escape.

The whistling tempest churned the tops off the waves, spraying the faces of the crew with stinging blades.

Oblivious to the severity of the storm, Bryce Sutton inspected his cargo by the light of a dim, handheld lantern. In the leaking, musty hold, the fifty special casks of wine sat tethered snugly together, jolting in unison as the ship crashed down from crest to trough. Some small amounts of water spurted into the bilges at each impact, but nothing of consequence. In fact, Sutton thought idly, there was less water in the hold than he had expected.

Turning toward the rear of the ship, Bryce congratulated himself for locating such a large amount of luxury items during wartime. Britain's involvement with the colonial rebellion had not diminished the market for finery. Two hundred boxes of perfume from Barcelona were packaged in thin cedar to resemble finely bound books. Each contained twelve vials of assorted exotic scents, and each would fetch a month's wages in the salons of London.

The thought of such a huge advance on his investment made Sutton smile. Remembering the fine quality silk, he strode toward the crates of fabric and opened one. Holding the lamp aloft with one hand, he plunged the other inside and immediately cursed angrily. The first bolt was swollen grotesquely with seawater. So was the next and the next. . . .

In a rage he turned from the bins. The seams of the brig were sprung. The cargo was soaked, perhaps ruined. Still thinking of lost profits, Sutton had not yet realized the true meaning of his discovery.

As he mounted the gangway, the groans of the ship could not conceal a distinct popping and cracking. Lurching against the handrails, he peered back into the dark space. As the ship slammed over another wave, wine casks burst from their moorings and rolled sternward. They bumped to a stop against the crates of silk and smashed into the delicate book-boxes of perfume. All shattered into a mound of splinters and reeking cloth.

Shouting again, Sutton climbed up to the cabin deck. His wife, Julia, was braced in the dark companionway near the bunks where the twins were lashed into immobility. Though Julia spoke soft, calming words to the infants, it was clear from her face that she was terrified of the raging weather outside. Lanterns had long before been extinguished for fear one might fall and cause a fire. The darkness and the moans of the ship's floundering shudders increased her apprehension.

"What's happened?" Julia's voice was quaking.

Her husband tried to sound composed. "The hold's a mess. Some casks broke free, and we've lost some of the perfume. Also part of the silk is wet, but I think it may be saved."

"*Saved!*" Julia said, panting. "This is insane. Why didn't we put in to the coast and make the crossing in the morning?"

"This weather was not supposed to be here," Sutton said reasonably. But the fact that he had to shout to make himself heard made his calm tone less than convincing.

William and Charles wailed louder as the brig heeled abruptly to port, then crawled crablike across the face of the wave before jolting upright again.

Sutton could hear more of the wine kegs breaking free and rolling, rapping the bulkheads beneath his feet. The wine had cost a pretty penny. Sutton hoped the cooper was worth his pay and that the barrels were sound.

Julia yelled something, but Sutton could not hear her until he leaned closer. "Is it too late, Bryce? Can't we turn back?"

"I trust Appiano," he roared. "He'll get us there."

"Perhaps we could put in to a cove on the coast of. . ."

"Of France! Who's insane now? Do you know what would happen to us if we were caught?"

Julia fell silent.

"All that wine," Sutton continued. "Silk, perfume . . . gone. A fortune handed over to the thieving French? Never!"

A sudden pitch knocked Sutton off his feet and threw him to the deck.

Julia helped her husband stand. "What good will a fortune be to us if we're dead?"

Sutton scowled in the darkness and turned away, holding both hands out to steady himself against the lurching of the ship. Ascending another gangway, he slid open a hatch cover and was immediately drenched with seawater. He gasped for breath at the unexpected iciness that froze his hands and face and plastered his dark hair across his forehead. He fought unsuccessfully to close the hatch until another lunge of the brig somersaulted him over it and secured the cover with a crash. Dazed, he clung to the wooden handgrip.

As he looked around, his face paled. The weather was much worse than he had imagined. His eyes widened as the *Hermes* was hoisted backward to the top of a thirty-foot swell and then slid downward into another trough. Sutton gripped the handle so tightly that his nails dug into his palm. Another wave loomed astern as the ship yawed awkwardly. Three sharp cracks came in quick succession. Cables whistled past his ear, and the mainmast leaned forward.

Captain Appiano caught sight of him from the helm station and lunged toward him. "Get below!" he ordered without his customary respect. "Do you want to be washed away? Get below and stay below!"

"We have to turn back. . . ."

"It's too late for that now!" Appiano returned. "The mainstays are gone, the mast itself may be next. . . . All is out of our hands!"

"Will we make it?"

When the captain did not respond, Sutton thought Appiano had not heard his question. He called louder, "WILL WE MAKE IT?"

"I don't know!" Appiano screamed as another wave pummeled *Hermes*. The impact knocked the captain down and broke, his hold on the lifeline. The gray-haired officer spun toward the port railing.

"Jonathan!" Sutton shouted, making an attempt to grasp the captain's elbow. A contrary roll of the ship flung him back the other direction and only by wrapping both hands around the hatch cover handle did he save himself. When the ship straightened, Sutton saw Appiano swept overboard. Two crewmen rushed toward the rail with a coil of line, but the captain had disappeared when Sutton struggled upright.

Bryce Sutton flung the hatch open and bellowed, "Julia! Julia!" Then as she responded from below he called, "Bring the boys ... leave everything else. Wait just below this hatch till I come back for you. Do it now!" He closed the cover again.

The *Hermes* heaved and shuddered her way to the top of another crest. To the east was a large dark mass ... land? "There!" he shouted to First Mate Vela. "Can we make that?"

"We can't put about in this sea without capsizing or foundering" was the reply.

"But what other choice have we?" Sutton insisted. "She could break apart any moment."

"And what of the French, sir?"

"Stop questioning me, and do as I say!"

Vela glared at his employer for a long second before giving the order to port the helm. The response was sluggish, angling the bow only slightly before another wall of water soaked the men.

"Sir," Vela warned, "we need to be prepared for the worst."

Sutton cut him short. "I know. I've told Julia to ready the children."

"I don't know how much longer she'll hold together. The keel timbers are already weak."

"Turn her toward land, Vela," Sutton yelled through gritted teeth.

As the ship fought her way perpendicular to the

onslaught of waves, another roller exploded against the hull and the *Hermes* floundered sideways.

"Idiot!" Vela shouted, abandoning the wheel. "There's no saving her now!"

"The lifeboat then? Will we be all right?"

"Better than if she sinks beneath us!"

The deck awash with three feet of green foaming water, the brig rolled on her side as if lying down to die. Sutton scrambled back toward the hatch as another wave broke over the starboard side and Vela shouted to the crew to get to the boats. Swimming instead of walking or crawling, Bryce Sutton overshot the hatch and was flung into the sea.

His wool suit dragged him downward and he shrugged out of the coat just as the broken cable of the mainstay snaked up out of the depths directly into his hands. Pleading with God to spare his family, Sutton erupted to the surface, his body numb with cold, his lungs on fire for breath.

The *Hermes* lay just before him, pummeled by the waves. To his amazement the brig fought to right herself one more time. His hands looped in a coil of line, Sutton was snapped forward and flicked against the aft hatch. As he reached for the handle, it opened to reveal Julia with a child under each arm. It was an odd moment to notice how beautiful she was and how strangely silent the children were.

The ship was settling lower in the water, the flooded rail only a foot from the surface. Above the foam he saw Vela struggling with the lifeboat and heard the mate shout, "Hurry before she rolls again!"

Reaching into the hatchway, Bryce took Charles from Julia's arms, then lifted his wife, together with his other son still in her embrace, bodily off the steps. Swinging her around him in an arc, he boosted mother and child into the lifeboat. Holding Charles high overhead out of the rush of water, Bryce Sutton bent to pass his second child into the boat.

At that moment the *Hermes* rolled yet again, throwing Sutton and Charles into the ocean. Kicking desperately for the surface, Sutton lifted the baby over his head and into the air. Sutton heard Julia calling his name above the screaming wind.

Something slammed into his shoulders from behind, making him cry out in pain. It was the aft-hatch cover, ripped free of its tracks and floating beside him, trailing a length of rigging. With his last ounce of strength, Sutton heaved himself and Charles aboard the tiny raft, tying a loop of rope around himself and the baby and through the handle. Feebly he waved toward the lifeboat. Someone . . . was it Julia? . . . pointed toward him, gesturing emphatically.

Then the biggest wave yet rolled over the settling brig. Her keelson timber snapping, the *Hermes* broke her back. The bowsprit folded toward the stern, and its beam hit Bryce Sutton squarely in the head. The hatch cover disappeared in a swirl of spume.

"No!" Julia screamed. "Find them! They must be alive! Please!"

"Please, ma'am," Vela insisted, forcing Julia down on a thwart. "They're gone . . . but we will be too if we don't get clear before she settles."

"They're not . . . we have to find them!"

Vela could see where the water frothed crimson with Bryce Sutton's blood. "If we're near the *Hermes* when she goes under, she'll suck us down." Giving a grim nod to the surviving crew members, Vela ordered them to pull away.

Julia sobbed, clutched William, and rocked him in her grief as the lifeboat drew apart from the foundering brig. As the small craft soared up to the crest of another wave, Julia could make out the ruins of the ship. The *Hermes* pitched, bow up, flinging spars wildly about as if signaling for help, before disappearing under the churning surf. Shattered wine casks and tiny bits of perfumed cedar bobbed in the foam to mark the place where the brig had been.

CHAPTER 1

Standing on tiptoe, Private Albert Penfeld craned his neck and strained his eyes, attempting to see across the forty miles of water that separated Boulogne from the south coast of England.

"Look!" his friend Cyrus Grieux exclaimed, pointing. "I can see the mastheads in Folkestone Harbor."

"You're crazy," Albert replied, brushing a lock of straight dark-brown hair out of his green eyes. "I can barely distinguish land from sea, let alone masts."

The two friends had followed the Rue de Strasbourg up from the harbor, climbing the high bluffs north of the city. Just now they were at the highest vantage point in the vicinity: the *cimetière du nord*.

Determined to prove his point, Cyrus hopped atop a stone sarcophagus bearing the family name of Duvalle, his bayonet-sheath flapping against his leg. "You see," he insisted, "it is a three-masted warship . . . a seventy-four gun, I think."

Albert joined his comrade atop the gravestone. "Bah!" he concluded in cordial skepticism. "Besides, why bother when the best view is this way?" Albert indicated the sweep of Boulogne-sur-Mer that lay below them.

Hundreds of invasion barges and transport ships were crammed into the boat basin. Galleys bearing freight, men, and messages scurried about the harbor like swimming water rats. Offshore a quartet of French frigates patrolled the mouth of the estuary, under the watchful heavy guns of the fort known as the *Haute Ville* and the headlands that ringed Boulogne.

On the far side of the harbor, in the direction of Henriville, lay the sprawling expanse of the Armèe de Angelterre; one hundred sixty thousand men waiting for the order that would launch the invasion of England. The timing of that order was, of course, everyone's favorite subject. "I feel it," Cyrus commented when he looked at the myriad campfires springing up in the fading light of early evening. "It will come soon. The emperor is back from Paris again, is he not? And since we know he will lead the attack personally, well, it follows that it must come soon."

Albert dug his elbow into Cyrus's ribs, knocking

him off his perch and onto the grassy slope. Cyrus's dark blue bicorne hat bounced end over end on the two points of its brim, threatening to roll clear down to the water. He scrambled after it, caught it, then returned, carefully brushing it free of sand and twigs. Resentfully he said, "You don't believe me, then?"

Laughing, Albert mocked him. "I believe you know the mind of the emperor just as strongly as I believe you can make out the ships in Folkestone Harbor. *Ma foi*, Cyrus, admit it: we have been here since March. It is now June. What makes it any more likely that the invasion will happen now than a week ago, or a month, except that we are that much more tired of waiting? Come on—if we are late back to picket duty, Sergeant Groffee will have our ears for a necklace."

Cyrus could not resist one more look across the tossing waves of La Manche, "the sleeve," which was naturally never referred to by its British name of *English Channel*. "Do you suppose that the English will fight with determination?"

"How can they?" Albert replied. "They don't like wine, and they drink beer by choice? *Faugh!*"

Since achieving supreme power as First Consul of France in 1799, Napoleon Bonaparte had forged the greatest military machine in the history of the world. He had used it to subjugate Italy, outmaneuver the Austrians, cow Bavaria into an alliance, effectively annex Spain, and isolate Great Britain. Having crowned himself emperor, by 1805 he was ready—eager in fact—to conclude the conquest of Europe by invading and neutralizing England. Only one force stood in his way: the Royal Navy.

Since March, Napoleon had been waiting for his combined fleet of French and Spanish warships to break out of the ports blockaded by the perfidious English. Whether they had to use force or subterfuge, he expected the arrival of the men-of-war off of Boulogne to escort the invasion armada to the Kentish shore.

In the meantime, one hundred sixty thousand men of the Grande Armèe grew bored, drank, fought duels, or deserted, as their characters demanded. Among these were Albert and Cyrus, conscripted out of the Latin Quarter of Paris, to serve beneath the gilt-bronze eagle of the Forty-sixth Line Regiment.

Just below the encampment of the army, and a mile from the main harbor, was an auxiliary boat basin known as the *Petit Port*. Until two days previous it had been the only remaining anchorage available to the fishing fleet of Boulogne since all the other space was reserved for the invasion ships. Then Napoleon, in his unending quest to bring overwhelming force to bear against the hated English, had requisitioned the Petit Port as well. The stone banks of its breakwater still supported piles of tangled nets, and the smell of rotting sardines hung heavily in the hot summer air.

Already more troop transports filled the moorings that had lately held fishing trawlers. As yet there had not been time to mount heavy cannons on the heights above the Petit Port, so the unmanned ships were guarded solely by Albert and his comrades of the Forty-sixth. Two batteries of field artillery were also in place on the wings of the quay.

As a thin sliver of moon chased the sun into La Manche, Albert and his fellow soldiers took up their dreary task of patrolling the Quai Sud. Their duty began at sunset and continued until two in the morning. *Four bells,* Albert reminded himself, trying to absorb maritime lore. Study had always been something he enjoyed. Indeed, he envied the students at the Sorbonne, not far from where he lived with his grandmother, Heloise. Many of the university pupils were also impoverished and struggled to make ends meet, but Albert, having no other family and no benefactor, had long since been apprenticed to Louis the tailor.

His Charleville musket carried at the slope in precisely regulation manner, Albert did his best in his service to the French empire. Joining had not even been his choice, let alone his desire, but he had determined to make the best of it. His agreeable nature had already been duly noted, and it was Cyrus's opinion that Albert would make corporal if the war lasted long enough.

It had lasted too long already as far as Albert was concerned. Apart from the out-of-reach dream of attending university, Albert's real goal was to earn enough francs to marry Angelique. Thoughts of her honey-blonde hair and athletic build were what carried him through the endless hours of picket duty.

Albert was wondering if he would see her again before the invasion was actually launched and he sailed for England. It was unlikely. He had not had a furlough since arriving at the coast, and Paris was days away on foot.

Nearing the eastern end of his one hundred assigned paces, Albert crossed paths with the next sentry, the hulking, kindhearted, but inept and ignorant Martin from Marseilles.

"*Bon soir,* Albert," Martin remarked for the fiftieth time that evening. "The wind is from the west."

"*Oui,*" Albert agreed—again. "It is blowing toward us from England."

Until Albert had spent some time with Martin, the young Marseillais had never learned compass points and had believed that the English were some rogue Frenchmen. Now Martin was so proud of his knowledge that he recited newly cherished facts at every opportunity.

Albert shared the stoppered gourd of water with his comrade. Canteens were not issued by the army, so it was up to every man to locate his own bottle. To Albert's knowledge, Martin had owned and lost six.

As Albert recovered the now-empty gourd and turned back toward the west, a shadow flitted across the breakwater from the ocean side toward the harbor. Albert was uncertain whether he had seen anything at all; the only light along the quay came from the flickering torches that marked the end of each sentry's circuit. Thus, the next circle of light to the west was some two hundred paces away. The observed movement, if such it had really been, was halfway between, in the darkest stretch of the rock wall.

Thinking that the shadow had been too big to be one of the thousands of rats in the port, Albert wondered what it could have been. Probably a trick of the light and his tired eyes. He considered calling for the corporal-of-the-guard, then remembered how Corporal Merchien hated being roused from his repose at the cozy guard shack. Albert did go so far as to unsling his weapon and check that there was still a charge of powder in the pan.

As nearly as Albert could make out, the faintly seen

activity had occurred near one of those heaps of abandoned netting and just beside an invasion barge named the *Gros Bec*. A six-foot-high mass of snarled webbing, two inches higher than Albert's own stature, loomed out of the darkness, merging into the still greater gloom of the ship.

At ten paces distant he halted to listen. A faint scraping sound reached him, and the back of his neck prickled. Then, along the line of his musket barrel, a cat meowed and Albert relaxed.

In the next second the night erupted into shadowy figures with blackened faces. Three clambered over the seawall from the ocean side and three more emerged from behind the netting.

The one of greatest concern for Albert was the one bearing down on him from a scant ten feet, brandishing a fiercesome boarding ax. With his bayonet-tip almost touching the attacker's chest, Albert pulled the trigger. The swing of the descending ax had already begun; it glanced off Albert's musket with enough force to almost knock it from his hands.

With Albert screaming for the corporal-of-the-guard at the top of his lungs, the remaining five assailants closed around him. He parried the blow of a cutlass with his bayonet, then clubbed the musket to drive another one back. "Hurry!" a voice hissed in English. "Finish him!"

Five were too many to resist successfully for long. Just as one cocked and aimed a dragoon pistol, another slipped inside Albert's guard with a cutlass. The heavy blade, more club than sword, slithered along Albert's musket just as the pistol exploded. The flat of the cutlass smacked against his forehead as a pistol ball pierced his left arm. He fell to the quay, nearly unconscious.

"That's done for 'im!" remarked the one who fired the shot. "Let's burn these tubs and 'ead for 'ome."

When Albert reawakened minutes later, shots were echoing all around the docks, and the *Gros Bec* was in flames. Despite the pains in his side and skull, Albert understood all: an English raiding party was attacking the Petit Port. They would burn or scuttle as many ships as they could and obstruct the harbor with the hulks.

When Albert pulled himself upright in the cover of the netting, the battle was raging westward on the embankment. The British were attempting to over-power the gun crew of one of the fieldpieces. As Albert hastily reloaded his musket, they succeeded in over-coming the guards, then wheeled the captured cannon around to face inward toward the harbor. The intent was clear: the attackers, rapidly running out of time, were going to use the French cannon to sink additional ships.

The fighting was taking place two ships farther down the quay, beyond another four-pounder fieldpiece that Albert remembered. Why had the English not used that weapon as well? His numb left arm dangling, Albert struggled along to the abandoned cannon.

That it had been fought over was evident by the four French bodies and one Englishman that lay all around and over the weapon. But why had the piece not been fired? Albert understood little about artillery, but he did know that in operation cannon were very similar to muskets.

Dragging the bloody form of an artillery captain off the barrel was not easy with one arm, nor was slewing the cannon around, yet Albert did so. He aimed the four pounder down the length of the breakwater and dumped the contents of his musket's priming pan into the touchhole. Then standing carefully to the side for fear of the recoil, he snapped his flintlock over the aperture.

At the last instant, Albert permitted himself a look at those he was about to annihilate. To his horror, the unmistakable hulking form of Martin loomed up in the middle of the English raiders around the cannon. Then the fire of the priming powder whooshed into the barrel, and the cannon exploded with a roar.

Although wary of the recoil, Albert had not reckoned on the fact that launching a cloth sack filled with four pounds of lead shot would cause the fieldpiece to buck like a horse rearing on its haunches. The cannon almost came over backward. Something struck Albert another blow on the head, and he slid downward into darkness.

It took several days for Albert to be able to stand upright without his head swimming. Although his wounded arm was painful and stiff and it was tied across his chest in a sling, it did not trouble him overly much. The regimental surgeon assured him there was no permanent damage to the muscle; he would soon recover its use.

On the fourth day following the attack by the English raiders, those who remained of Albert's company were paraded before the chateau of the *Haute Ville,* the residence occupied by the emperor himself. The Forty-sixth received a commendation for repelling the assault. Although two transport ships had been burned, quick action had prevented the flames from spreading to the rest of the harbor. Moreover, the damaged ships were towed out of the Channel to sink, leaving the port unobstructed. All the attacking party, who were found to have come from an English frigate anchored a few miles south, were either captured or killed.

Albert's action with the cannon had accounted for a dozen of the raiders and was held to be the single moment that had turned the tide of battle. For that reason he was standing three paces in front of his regiment as the emperor addressed them.

"Children . . . my children . . . ," Napoleon called to them from the terrace of the chateau. His round face was shining, and his hair, combed straight forward, gleamed with the lavender pomade he favored. "You have seen how the English choose to fight: by night, in disguise, and not like proper soldiers at all! But you have shown yourselves to be more than their equals. You are the superior men in all ways. It only remains for you to carry the war to their shores as they have seen fit to attack ours. And I . . . I shall be proud to lead you myself!"

Three times three huzzahs of approval greeted these words and then the emperor called for Albert to ascend the stairs and join him on the balcony. When Albert had done so, Napoleon loudly proclaimed, "And this is the very embodiment of your fighting spirit! Even wounded he carried on the fight, single-handedly firing the shot that swept the enemy from our presence, just as I swept the royalist mob from the boulevard during the Revolution. It seems his motto must be the same as my own: give them a whiff of grapeshot!"

There was boisterous laughter at this sign of camaraderie.

"There remain two things . . . Albert Penfeld, I award you the order of the Legion of Honor." Here the emperor hung the scarlet ribbon and jeweled cross around Albert's neck and pressed his lips against both of Albert's cheeks. Then he added, "For such a man, only opportunity for greater glories will satisfy. You may choose one of the elite services, and I will transfer you at once, excepting only the Imperial Guard."

Permitted to speak for the first time, Albert responded softly, "Majesty, I am not worthy of so great an honor. Besides, how can I leave my comrades?"

"True nobility!" Napoleon announced to the assembly. "He wishes to share his distinction with all of you. But I cannot dispense with all of the magnificent Forty-sixth; however, he may choose one of his comrades to accompany him."

About to refuse a second time, Albert saw the pleading expression on Cyrus's face. It was clear Cyrus still saw the war as a path to fame and privilege, and so he nodded his acceptance.

"And what service shall you choose?" the emperor inquired.

Marshall Berthier, Napoleon's chief-of-staff, hissed, "Artillery . . . say 'the artillery.'"

Again Albert looked to Cyrus for guidance and saw his friend look very pointedly at a uniformed cavalryman drawn up in the guard of honor.

"Your Majesty," Albert replied, "I choose the cavalry. The hussars."

Napoleon's lower lip jutted out in a momentary pout, then composing his features he said quickly, "Very well, you and your comrade are now members of the First Hussars. Wear your new uniform with as much distinction as you did the last."

And Napoleon swept away without any further comment.

Berthier muttered, "Young fool! The emperor gave you the clue when he reminded everyone that he was in the artillery. Had you only half a brain your fortune would have been made!"

But Cyrus, much more sanguine, exulted in their good fortune. "The First Hussars! The very souls of swagger and dash! Women will throw themselves at us! *Ma foi*, Albert, our lives have just improved a thousandfold!"

Of all the assembly, it seemed that only Albert himself was without a strong preference for fame and fortune and glamour. He could not help thinking over and over how if he had seen Martin in time, he would never have fired the blast from the cannon at all.

CHAPTER 2

A few thick, violet clouds loomed near a moon full to bursting, its white sheen illuminating everything below. The dank smell of marsh, moss, and reed thickened the feel of the night.

Buzzing in the humid air above Hampstead Heath, a thousand crickets' refrain was interrupted by the clopping of iron-shod hooves and the metallic chatter of bridle with bit. As by the wave of a conductor's baton, all the clamor ceased in a single instant.

Drifting downward from the summit of the hill that loomed four miles from the heart of London, the cheery noises of human celebration echoed back to the approaching rider. He and the crickets paused to listen, then both resumed their use of that summer evening in England in 1805.

Galloping forcefully up the badly rutted road to the

top of the heath, the traveler noted how the voices grew louder. Lantern lights appeared, sparkling through the drooping limbs of the elms that encircled the summit. With a flick of his riding crop the traveler urged his mount to still greater speed, dodging and cutting among the trees with energy and intent.

Inside the confines of the pub known as Jack Straw's Castle, the doubtful music of many a well-lubricated throat overflowed to the tune of "Blind Willie":

> *And when he's hampered in the dust,*
> *still will his fame be springin',*
> *for times we run till like to bust,*
> *to hear Blind Willie singin'!*

Skidding to a sudden halt on the cobbled forecourt, the rider dismounted before the horse could even stagger forward to regain its balance. In the light that poured out of the wide-open windows of the pub, the traveler was seen to be in his twenties, strongly built, above middle height, with dark hair, a square jaw, solid shoulders, and an arrogant set to his head. He flung his riding cloak back as an elderly hostler took the reins from him. Reaching into the pocket of his leather breeches, he pulled out a coin and dropped it into the hand of the crookbacked attendant.

"Harf a crown!" the groom exclaimed. "Blimey! That's more'n two weeks' wages!"

"Yes, it is," the gentleman replied.

"Very generous, indeed, sor! Goin' ta hazard a great pile as well?"

"Win!" the rider corrected. "Win a great pile! Indeed I shall. And all I ask of you is that you take good care of this animal for me. A measure of oats, if you please, and rub him down with clean straw."

"Jack's best," the hostler retorted with the time-honored jest. "His lordship may rely on me!" The man smiled toothlessly, pulling a forelock that consisted of three strands of white hair. "Thank you, again, my lord! And good luck to you!"

The gentleman waved away the gratitude as if the money meant nothing. Just before the round-topped plank door he stopped to adjust the white linen stock around his throat, then swung the portal wide open. It crashed against the wall inside, drawing curious looks from the mixture of common and well-to-do patrons that frequented Jack Straw's. The latecomer swaggered in, totally disregarding the attention his arrival generated. But most of the clientele went quickly back about their business, and the laughter and the singing continued uninterrupted.

However, one man at the bar did not return to his

pint. Instead he stared insolently at the newcomer. "Oy, innkeeper," he squawked. The speaker, a coarse-looking brute with thick arms, thick neck, and thick lips, jerked his head with a shake of dirty blond hair. Impatiently he thumped the publican on the back. "Who in blazes is that fancy bloke? You answer Bristol Sims when he asks you sommat."

The tavern keeper, a thin, nervous-eyed Londoner, answered, "That is William Charles Sutton." Barman and drinker both studied the man spoken of as he passed through the crowd. Contained within the respectfully uttered name was a great deal more information: William Charles Sutton, grandson of Lord Randolph Sutton, and heir to the second-largest shipping concern in all of Britain.

"That's 'im?"

"Aye," the diminutive host agreed. "Wagers away more in one night than a plowman's life is worth."

Sims watched with mingled envy and hatred as the crowd parted for Sutton at a wave of his hand. Sims turned his head, spat heavily on the floor, then sneered again.

His drinking companion, a fat, sweaty, red-nosed dolt with the unlikely name of Nick Chopper, chuckled. "I know . . . 'e thinks 'e's Moses! Partin' the waters, see? Like Moses."

"Shut yer gob," Sims growled. "I'm thinkin'."

The innkeeper tilted his head and cocked one eye. "Aye, young Sutton could've bought the tavern twenty times over with the money 'e's lost in 'ere."

This repeated information penetrated Bristol Sims's thick skull. "Come here much, does he?"

The tavern master considered. "Been away of late, but reg'lar before that. Seems 'e's quite taken with my barmaid. Judy's 'er name."

Now Sims's face swelled with venom. "I know Judy well, but she ain't never said nothin' 'bout little Lord Sutton."

The innkeeper started. Looking around nervously he answered, "I seen 'em together, but I can't tell ye ought more." Then he moved deliberately away from Sims to refill a pitcher of ale.

Chopper roared with laughter. "Bristol! That wench a yours been dancin' to someone else's tune!"

Slamming his mug on the floor where it shattered with a crash, Sims's hands clutched the air as if in search of a neck to throttle. Beginning with Chopper, those nearby edged quickly out of reach. "Where's that tart?" Sims shrieked, storming off in search of Judy.

In a room at the rear of the pub, a crowd of excited men and their female companions flocked around a wooden barricade encircling a sawdust-covered ring.

The shouting, gesturing gamblers exchanged coins and bills for scraps of paper. In the middle of the pit was a stocky Welshman wearing a cloth riding cap and holding a black-and-white terrier. The handler stroked the dog's ears as the animal whined and struggled in his grasp.

In the middle of the mob, and yet not part of it, was William Sutton. As soon as his presence was noted, the oddsmaker stopped accepting two-shilling bets and approached the young lord. "Care to wager, yer lordship?"

"What is the count?"

"Twenty-five, my lord," said the oddsmaker, gesturing at a slate under a brick arch on which the number was displayed alongside the words *Three minutes*.

William smiled. "Indeed." Reaching deep into his pocket, he pulled out a stack of gold sovereigns.

The little oddsmaker became flustered. "I can't cover all that! She's favored."

William shook his head. "Against, my good man, against. I have seen many a terrier catch rats, but even the dashing Dagmar cannot cope with twenty-five country rats in three minutes."

"Done!" the oddsmaker shouted, exchanging a marker for the coins.

William Sutton watched as the bets were completed, and the oddsmaker raised his arm in a call for silence. "Scorekeeper ready?" he bellowed.

"Ready!" called a young fellow by the chalkboard.

"Dog ready?"

The Welshman holding the dog nodded confidently, climbed out of the ring, and suspended the quivering terrier in midair.

The oddsmaker-turned-announcer made a great show of displaying a pocketwatch as big as the palm of his hand. "The wager is twenty-five rats in three minutes!" Stepping out of the ring, he warned, "On my mark then!"

Another assistant raised a wire cage filled with terrified, screeching rats and held it poised over the lip of the ring. He emptied the container with a flourish, shaking loose twenty-five large rodents to scurry and leap around the pen.

The Welshman kissed the dog on top of the head and mouthed the words, "To it now, sweet."

"Ready. . . . Steady. . . ." The announcer threw his head back. "Go!" he cried, swinging his arm toward the floor.

Dagmar the ratter was thrown halfway across the ring, where she scrambled after the fleeing rats, quickly catching one in mid-leap. The dog gave a violent shake of her head and in less than a second pitched the first body down and was onto another. In a frenzy the terrier ripped into rat after rat, accounting for fifteen before half the allotted time was gone.

Counting the remaining rats, William was still confident he would win, since the terrier now had to cover more ground between kills and twice grabbed already dead rats in error. Then too, she seemed to be slowing, and Dagmar shook her head against the painful bites she had received on her ears and lips from the rats.

Then as the rats scurried in seemingly random flight, three of them suddenly collided, and before they could escape, all were scooped up and dispatched by the dog. Five more were vanquished in quick succession.

William choked in dismay. The crowd went wild, cheering and beating the sides of the pen. The dog shot across to grab another when William looked at the clock.

The timer began to count aloud, "Ten, nine, eight. . ."

William spun his gaze back to the action where there was only one rat left. "Curse you, animal," he growled with gritted teeth.

The timer continued. "Five, four. . ."

When the count reached three the feisty Dagmar snapped at the last of twenty-five rats with a flourish and flung it aside with two seconds to spare. The men of the pub erupted into a cheer, clamoring over one another and waving.

"Blast it!" William swore under his breath, crumpling the scrap of paper.

"William!" a voice called.

Turning to look, Sutton spotted a young man of middling frame, fair skin, light-brown hair and pale-blue eyes. "Thomas, my good man! Fancy seeing you here!"

"Did you see the sport?"

William smiled carelessly. "Surely," he said, crossing his arms. "Have you ever known me to miss a chance for a bit of excitement?"

Thomas Burton's eyes lit up. "Excellent! It calls for celebration." He grinned broadly. "And you're buying."

"Your conclusions are too hasty indeed."

Thomas looked puzzled.

"I fear I backed the rats."

"Oh!" Thomas groaned. "Foolish man! To throw away money like that . . . and more than was wise, knowing you! And I thought your allowance was curtailed."

"And so it is," William replied, waving his hands at his sides in a show of careless resignation. "It's only money. There'll be plenty more where that came from."

His comment seemed to satisfy Thomas's concerns.

Reentering the bar area, Thomas pulled up a chair for William before sitting down himself. "Ale for both of us," Thomas ordered. "So tell me of these voyages from which you've newly returned. Exciting new lands and strange and exotic women. Spain, I think."

"And North Africa. Desolate place . . . nothing fit to eat or drink the entire time. The voyage took two weeks. It was quite unnerving to think about all of the warships on the seas at this moment. We made not a single stop on the return and raced past all the capes thought to be infested by French vessels. Once we spotted a sail veering to intercept our course, but we outsailed them till sunset and then lost them. Nuisance, really, nothing more."

Thomas became excited. "Nothing more? What about Bonaparte? William, the entire country is in a positive lather about Boney and the invasion. They say he may strike at any time. What about your captain? Was he an old salt, a man well decorated?"

William Sutton sniffed as if the subject were of little interest. "Of course. Only the best for my grandfather's ships. You've heard of him, no doubt: Collins, a war hero discharged after losing a leg in American waters during the time of the colonial rebellion. Seems he stayed at his post and refused to strike his colors. Saved his ship because of it. Ponderous old buffer . . . has no head for liquor or cards . . . frightfully boring, actually."

"They say he was a tenacious warrior . . . much like

that terrier just now. It has always impressed me the things a man will do for his country in battle. Perhaps we shall soon have a chance to show what we are made of ourselves!"

"Foolish, if you ask me," William snapped. "Sorry, Thomas, but I'd have let the vessel sink. He might have kept his leg!"

Thomas nodded slowly as if weighing a response. At last he said, "William, I have important news!" Thomas leaned forward, clenching his hands together. Taking a deep breath, he said, "I have received a commission as lieutenant of the Royal Marines with Admiral Nelson. I'm to sail aboard the *Agamemnon*."

William cleared his throat and looked around as if he were distracted. Nodding he replied, "Well, that's wonderful then, yes. There you have it. A real-life marine."

Despite his friend's obvious lack of enthusiasm, Thomas could hardly hold back his smile. "Yes! To get Old Boney by the throat and thrash him like a rat!"

"Ah," William added, "you and the famous Lord Nelson. Hero of the Battle of the Nile. Defend Britannia's shores and all that. Good show, old man."

"And how about you then?" Thomas inquired. "Has Admiral Cornwallis come 'round to speak with you yet?"

William sipped his drink and made a sour face

before answering regretfully, "Tomorrow. I see him tomorrow. My grandfather insists."

"But that's splendid." Thomas searched his friend's eyes. "Isn't it? Lord Cornwallis is commander-in-chief of the Channel Fleet. He could arrange for us to be shipmates."

In the silence that followed this declaration, William understood that Thomas knew the truth. "It is nothing I want to do. It's what my grandfather wants for me. Let him go fight the French himself, I say!"

"But think of the fame, the glory," Thomas argued.

"Look at me, Thomas." William gestured toward himself. "Do I look like I lack money? No. Then what care I for fame?"

"But above all think of the adventure!"

"Well enough for some," William said, sighing. "But not what I want."

"Enough for tonight then," Thomas said, unwilling to be at odds with his best friend so soon after his return. Slapping William on the shoulder, Thomas invited, "You must hear about this girl I'm seeing! She's absolutely brilliant and plays the piano as well as any I ever heard. I was with her all day today and am going to meet her tonight."

William instantly warmed to the new subject. "You sly devil. . . . Well, speaking of ladies," he said and winked. He motioned behind Thomas toward a beautiful young woman with fiery red hair and sparkling green eyes that boldly looked every man in the face.

Thomas spun back around to face him. "Another barmaid, William? Then I can see my presence is unnecessary. I am off." Thomas reached out to shake his friend's hand. "Good luck on your big day tomorrow. And may you find whatever it is you are really looking for . . . true love?"

William smiled back. "That's absurd. I seek nothing beyond the moment." He pondered the thought. "No, I don't see love as part of this relationship."

Thomas shook his head. "Tell me no more, else I'll have a guilty conscience."

"I won't," William called out. "You see the very example of the perfect balance of our friendship, Thomas. You the guilt, and me the pleasure!"

Thomas walked off, raising his hand in farewell. "Till tomorrow, then."

William downed the last of his drink and rushed off to intercept the lovely Judy. Even in the dimness of the pub she was radiant. When she turned slowly around, the revolution of William's world wound to a dead stop. As she smiled at him, William felt a fire begin to gnaw at his insides. No woman had ever made him afraid, yet somehow Judy made him tremble.

"Hello, William," she greeted him, smiling seductively while presenting a cheek toward him.

William fought back an urge to grab her with both arms and kiss her. "Good evening, Judy. You look incredibly beautiful. Such a sunrise as you belongs not on an earth so gray and colorless as this."

She thanked him with a direct gaze and the words, "Aren't you going to kiss me?"

He gave in to his desires, wrapping his arms tight around her. Pulling her close, he kissed her long and hard, inhaling deeply of the aroma of rosewater. In the musty, smoky atmosphere of the pub, her smell was like a field of flowers. "Come with me," he murmured into her ear.

Pushing him away and laughing, Judy demanded, "Gamble for me, William."

He knew her well enough to know he must humor her mood.

In a corner of the room was a group playing at hazard. William drew a pouch of gold from his coat. Briefly he weighed it and the consequences, a distant warning bell ringing in the back of his mind. Then Judy rubbed warmly against his arm, and he tossed the sack onto the playing table.

The wager was a simple one. William was betting that the sum of three throws of the dice would total more than eighteen. There was one additional stipulation, however: the three casts could not include any doubles, or the proposition was lost immediately.

William offered the dice to Judy to kiss, then carelessly flung them onto the counter. He was so absorbed in thoughts of the young woman that he neither looked at the throw, nor did he at first hear the result. "What did you say?" he asked in disbelief.

"I said, you have lost, my lord."

Looking downward, William was stared back at by a pair of black, unblinking dots.

"It's not possible. That money I . . ." William's head was spinning and he let the feeling carry him away from the table. "Well," he said at last. "It seems I've already lost all I had tonight."

"All!" Judy repeated in disbelief.

"All," he repeated firmly. He sat down and dropped his head into his hands.

He did not even look up when she said, "William, this is most unmanly, and not like you at all. Let's not let this ruin our night."

"You don't understand!"

"Yes, I do. It was a lot of money."

"That's not all." He faced her. "It wasn't even my money."

"What?"

"It was my grandfather's money. It was the earnest money for new sails that must be made for one of his ships."

Judy listened without speaking.

"I've got to get it back somehow. . . ." William squinted in consternation, running his hands through his hair. "I'll have to borrow it or maybe say I lost the money or that I was robbed, perhaps?"

"Oh, no!" Terror gripped her expression. "How could you do such a thing?"

"That's beside the point now!" he yelled, gripping her by the arms. "Just leave me alone awhile. If your credit is good here, then get me a bottle . . . or steal one. In fact, get two!"

Judy edged away.

Money for the new sails, he thought to himself. "Blast it!"

At that moment a pair of legs like tree trunks pushed into his vision and two fingers poked William in the chest. William bounded upright.

"I been watchin' you, see," Bristol Sims said in a menacing tone. "And I seen ye with my Judy."

"And who the devil are you?"

"Him who is gonna smart you up in a way ye 'aven't learned yet!"

William looked the fellow up and down. "Your

Judy!" He laughed. "I certainly didn't see her kissing you tonight. But on the other hand, you may be right. What did you say your name was again?"

"Sims. Bristol Sims."

"Sims, yes. I think I do remember Judy speaking of you before. In fact she spoke quite a lot of you."

Sims looked baffled.

"Take her," William said. "She's yours."

Sims looked disgusted and disappointed at having been deprived of a chance to educate William Sutton. He shoved William once more for good measure, then stalked off, gloating.

Judy hurried back to William's side, carrying two bottles of port wine. "Was that Bristol Sims? What happened? What did he say to you?"

Snatching the bottles out of the young woman's hands, William said, "Sorry to cut the evening short. Must go . . . sure you understand."

Judy nodded and asked, "When will I see you again?"

"Soon, I hope . . . soon," he replied more firmly. "Good night."

Near the door were a trio of hard-drinking drovers, lean men who kept to themselves. William Sutton stopped beside the biggest of the three. "Do you know who I am?" he asked softly.

"Aye" was the gruff response. "What of it?"

"Do you know an ape who calls himself Bristol Sims?" William persisted. This was answered in the affirmative by a squint of the eyes. "A half crown for the three of you if you beat him to a pulp and throw him in a ditch. Here's a bottle to seal the bargain. Come to Sutton Hall the day after tomorrow, and you'll be paid."

Half the contents of the other bottle went down William's throat before he had completed the ride back to his grandfather's Hampstead manor house, though it was only a mile away.

CHAPTER 3

———⸙———

The manor house belonging to the Sutton family stood atop a high plateau on Hampstead Heath. Built of brick in the year of the Great Fire of 1666, the home was an imposing structure possessing eight bedrooms and a view all the way down to the dome of St. Paul's cathedral. The waters of the spa at Hampstead no longer attracted the quality, given the new fashions of traveling to Bath or Tunbridge Wells, but this change suited Lord Randolph Sutton completely. In point of fact, he never considered buying property in Hampstead until the day-trippers ceased making it their destination of choice.

William walked briskly away from the stable. Leaving behind the narrow gravel path that circled a hedge-enclosed garden, he trotted across a lush lawn. Despite the glories of the place William hardly noticed all the wonderful sensations of sight, sound, and smell that so grand an English garden could boast in high summer. His thoughts, far from the flowers and the birds singing, carried in two wildly different directions at once. The scent of roses blooming made him think of Judy—this subject he would have been content to dwell on. Unfortunately, the other person occupying William's mind was Admiral Cornwallis.

Having seen the admiral's carriage arrive a half hour earlier, William had been thinking of reasons to avoid reentering the house. This desire was in turn counterbalanced by William's worry over his grandfather's displeasure and the yet undisclosed gambling loss of company funds.

Sweat rolled down from William's forehead and onto his cheeks. He grabbed the loose ends of his neckerchief and wiped the drops from his flushed face. Realizing how disarranged this left his appearance, he attempted to correct his mistake by shaking out the damp stock and cinching it back high and tight around his neck.

Making his way into the servants' entry, William successfully pushed unseen through a double swinging door into a hall behind his grandfather's study. From within that room he could hear voices. One was the dominating baritone of his grandfather, always one notch louder in volume than necessary as though still personally in command of the sailing ship with which he had begun his career.

The second voice, though not as familiar, was without a doubt the reedy treble of Admiral William Cornwallis. Although he was the brother of the general widely blamed for losing America to the rebels, Admiral Cornwallis was admired and had been given authority over all British warships in the home waters of the Channel. It was about that very duty that William was overhearing.

"I tell you, Randolph, Old Boney is chafing to land his invasion fleet on our shores, has been for months," Cornwallis asserted. "If we fail to keep the combined Franco-Spanish fleet bottled up in Spain they will rendezvous with the troop transports waiting just across the Channel. And then, God help us, there will be fighting in Kent before the end of August."

"Balderdash," Lord Sutton retorted. "Everyone knows that the shooting season does not properly begin until the first day of September. Even the Frogs would not be so unmannerly as to break such an old tradition." Silently William urged his grandfather on, but apparently Lord Sutton's argument was only the banter between old friends because he continued in a more somber tone, "Do you think it will come to that?"

"Pon my honor, Randolph, it is every whit that serious. Why, the county militias are being raised all over the south and east."

Both men harrumphed loudly at the mental image of country bumpkins marching with pitchforks and spades to repel the legions of Napoleon's Grand Armée. Those same French troops had already placed Bonaparte in full control of Europe from Spain to Austria.

"Surely our brave lads of the Home Fleet will never let the crossing take place," Grandfather Sutton suggested. "Nelson will thrash the French admiral Villeneuve soundly."

"But the attempted breakout will be made," Cornwallis returned. "And it must come before the season is too advanced for campaigning. Now is the time for a young man to cover himself in glory. Prime opportunity that may not come again in our lifetime. And speaking of young men, where is your grandson? You had me come all the way out here to get a look at a new second lieutenant, and he's not here."

William thought seriously about slipping back out the rear door and had even gone so far as to turn in that direction when the floor creaked under his feet. He barely had time to put an ingratiating smile on his features before the study door burst open, and his grandfather accosted him.

"There you are!" Lord Sutton cried. "Where have you been? Admiral Cornwallis has been waiting three quarters of an hour."

"I know, and I regret it very much," William said with a bow toward the uniformed and decorated admiral. "Matters of business relating to the new sails kept me. My apologies." Then, attempting to take control of the conversation, he stated, "Admiral, I am looking forward to joining the campaign next spring. Quite taken with the notion, actually."

The admiral shook his head in a manner reminiscent of a wet dog, blinked his watery eyes, and blurted, "Next spring! What do you mean, next spring? There's a war on now! Lord Randolph's letter suggested you would be ready to serve at once!"

Intimidated by the force with which the man spoke, William responded, "My grandfather is thinking of my future prospects and what a glorious opportunity this is, but I cannot leave him at a time when the needs of the shipping concern are so great. No, no. No matter how much I might want to serve, it would not be right."

The surprised look of gratitude William saw on his grandfather's face encouraged him to speak more boldly. So he blurted something he immediately regretted. "Besides, I am the last of the Suttons. And as you say, there is a war on. I find it might be a terribly easy time for one to get killed."

The admiral looked dumbfounded. "What?!! What more glorious end could one desire than to die for God and country?"

William searched for the words that would save the situation before it was too late. "Yes, dying is all well and good, Admiral, but I just don't think dying is for me, not right now. What I mean to say is, it's a wonderful opportunity, but . . . but what would happen to Grandfather if I were killed?" he concluded lamely.

Lord Randolph rubbed the wrinkles on his forehead as he stared at the parquet floor. His cheeks reddened with every word that William spoke; even his commanding voice deserted him.

Admiral Cornwallis turned to the elder Sutton with a sour look on his face. He spoke as if William were not even in the room. "I thought you said the lad had turned into quite a man." Lord Randolph's explanation was cut short. "Don't bother. In light of our friendship, Randolph, I will not use the word *coward*, but my position makes me assert this: I know a potential deserter when I see one. Easy time to get killed, indeed. Good day to you, sir."

Cornwallis stormed out of the house while Grandfather Sutton hung his head in shame. "How could you say such things, William?"

"Now, Grandfather," William began. "I am just starting to make myself useful—to the business, I mean. Why should I go off to play at..."

A sharp downward gesture of Randolph Sutton's hand stopped William's excuses. "You lack discipline, William. I thought the service would make a man of you. I was prepared to buy you—yes, buy—your commission, to give you that chance. Now you have thrown it away. Lord Cornwallis would not have you as an officer on a ship of the line for any amount of money. I shall have to think of something else."

It had been a long time since William had seen his grandfather so upset. Lord Sutton got right in his face, almost standing on William's toes so as to get that much closer when he yelled. "Now when I have, somehow, by the grace of God, managed to find something else for you, I suggest you do not discard it lightly. There will be nothing more from the House of Sutton until you have proven yourself. Do you understand?"

William swallowed hard. "Yes, sir."

Grandfather Sutton stared, nostrils flaring, waiting for even the smallest sign of disagreement from William. When it did not come, he relaxed a bit and paced over to the fireplace. Picking up a small wooden model of a three-masted West Indies trader, he studied its every detail. "And what of your responsibilities to refit *Stronghold*? When will the sailcloth be ready?"

Sensing an opportunity for renewing his grandfather's respect, William reported, "I have made contact with Master Hall, as you instructed. He has given me the figures for a complete replacement of the canvas, but. . ." William paused awkwardly, remembering the money lost. "But according to Hall, due to the required canvas for the navy, there is some question that it can be done in a timely manner."

"What does that mean?" Lord Randolph inquired dryly.

"I believe three months was mentioned." Grandfather Sutton appeared ready to explode again, so William hastily added, "I knew that was impossible, so I took the liberty of contacting another firm, Helmsteder and Company. Unfortunately they are somewhat more expensive, and they expect the entire payment in advance."

"All of it? That has never been required before."

"Mister Helmsteder says the demand for sailcloth is so great that it must be cash-and-carry." Now that William had successfully diverted his grandfather's thoughts from his own shortcomings to the condition of the nation in wartime, William knew it was time to get away. He crept to the doorway.

"You're off then?"

"Yes, to speak with Thomas about some urgent matters—target practice as well."

"And what matters are these?"

"Uh," William said as he thought quickly, "he has accepted an appointment as an officer of the marines and wishes to speak with me about it."

"Good!" Lord Randolph said with approval. "Thomas is a young man of character, not like your other acquaintances. But I'll say no more. By all means, hear him out."

William responded carefully, "I won't disappoint you, sir."

Grandfather Sutton did not look convinced of the sincerity behind William's words. "Life," he said, "is too short for regret and can be painfully long if the regret is inescapable. Stop thinking about disappointing me, William, and see if your own heart is satisfied with who you are. But when did the young ever listen to the warnings of the old before falling on their faces first?" Lord Randolph abruptly abandoned his reverie. "Oh, and William, you will be attending divine services with us tomorrow. Your mother says she feels well enough to make the attempt. I know you will not fail her."

William paused in the hallway, searching for an excuse, though the notice had been delivered as an order.

"You *will* join us for church tomorrow," his grandfather insisted.

"I'll be there," William promised regretfully. "Good day to you, sir."

The woods were full of chattering magpies and the soft mournful calls of doves. The pond resounded with the honking of a flock of geese. Thomas Burton secured the stock of his musket tight to his shoulder and carefully clicked the flintlock hammer into place. Breathing in deeply and holding it, he set his sights on the distant round of red-painted wood. Squinting his left eye shut, he froze in place, tightening his grip around the stock and trigger. He was taking an immense amount of care with this shot, unwilling to concede the contest to William.

Ever so gently he squeezed, until, with a rush, the hammer fell and the chip of flint struck the plate, igniting a tiny spark. The noise of the birds was silenced by an immensely loud boom, and a cloud of black smoke drifted past William as the peal rang back from the green countryside.

"Oh, drat!" Thomas exclaimed. "I can never hit the target from this distance."

William rested his hand on his friend's shoulder and leaned forward to look. "Don't be so hard on yourself, old man. I think you nicked the corner of the log underneath it."

Thomas jabbed him in the ribs. "Mind your manners! Let us see if you can hit Old Boney from a hundred long paces."

"It's really not that far," William retorted, grabbing the heavy, octagonally barreled weapon and removing the slender wooden ramrod. "I've made farther shots hit bumble bees." William jumped quickly aside, dodging a second swipe at his ribs.

"All mouth, I wager. Let's see you hit it a second time."

William cleared the musket of fouling, refilled the pan, measured out a cap of powder, about a teaspoon's worth, and plugged it down tight with a lead ball the size of a marble. All these motions were made so deliberately that Thomas knew he was being taunted, and he in turn teased his friend.

Then just as Thomas opened his mouth to urge William to get on with it, William snapped the weapon into place. Disregarding the obnoxious comments Thomas murmured in his ear, ignoring the squawks of the geese, and scorning the fact that the sun had disappeared behind a cloud, William fired after less than a single second's aim.

The bullet whizzed past the marshy pond, striking the center of the target. The target jumped off the log like a loose wheel jolted from a carriage at high speed. It spun into the tall grass and came to rest thirty feet away.

Thomas began to speak but was hushed by William. "*Shhh*," he urged. "Don't you hear that?"

Thomas frowned, straining to listen. "What?"

William jabbed him hard in the stomach. "The sound of the crowd cheering my victory."

Unready for the attack, Thomas gasped. "Easy now! My supper has not digested yet."

William handed him back the rifle and commented sarcastically, "Better get used to it. There won't be a lot of time for that when you're on the ship either. It'll be yes sir, aye aye, sir, please kick me again, sir. Never a time for a proper meal. Oh, Thomas, must you join the marines? It all sounds so drear."

They walked past the heaping green mound of hayricks toward a little dirt trail, Thomas deep in thought. "Have joined," he corrected. "I have already joined. So really, what is it you have against the military? You were raised around ships. You are a crack shot, you give instruction with humor, you are used to issuing commands and having them obeyed. You are a natural to become an officer and a leader of men."

William snorted. "Not me! Oh, I admit to having had boyhood dreams—that sort of thing. You hear the stories about pirates and their buried treasure and then the gallant captain, the story's hero," he said, turning to Thomas and waving an imaginary sword, "comes along and takes it back, saves the beautiful princess, and returns to England after sinking the pirate ship with cannon-fire."

"And what is wrong with that, I might ask?" Thomas said, smiling.

"It's not that there is anything wrong with the story, but if you intend using that as a matter for planning a lifelong career, you are a candidate for Bedlam Hospital. What about all the things that were too boring for the writer to leave in the story? That's why they were cut: 'Here, mate, eat that swill and like it. Polish those buttons and my boots too while you're about it.' No thank you, Thomas," William concluded. "If someone wanted to make me admiral of the blue my first cruise, then I'd tip my hat and say 'Thank'ee,' but otherwise, give me my freedom. Can you imagine me having to toady up to some idiot officer just because he is an officer? And to make matters worse, it's every day, all day, on and on."

William broke into the imagined voices of naval officer and midshipman. "Boy!" he shouted. "Get my glass! Aye aye, sir. Get my charts! Aye aye, sir. Empty my chamber pot. With pleasure, sir. I mean, honestly, Thomas!"

Holding up his hands in token of surrender, Thomas conceded the point. "You are right. Your disruptive presence on a British man-of-war would be too much comfort for Napoleon. Anyway, I must dash. I'm to board ship at Portsmouth."

William grew serious at the last. "Take care of yourself, Thomas. You are the best friend I have, and for all your high-mindedness, and perhaps because of it, you are the only one I fully trust."

"God be with you, William."

CHAPTER 4

———⚜———

In Albert's mind, the best result of his transfer to the hussars was the leave to go home. But he still felt conspicuous in his sky-blue, red-trimmed uniform with its tall hat and plume. He was conscious of many stares and questions and seriously considered discarding the cavalryman's rig until his return to camp.

Leading a nondescript bay horse of some age, Albert walked down the Rue St. Jacques in Paris, gazing up the tall buildings that overhung the street. The odor of the city was almost unbearable after the clean salt air of the seacoast. Sewage ran in open drains down the center of the street, and nearby a fishmonger peddled his drying wares, which only contributed to the stench.

Never before had Albert noticed what a shambles he grew up in. He remembered his childhood as a happy one, even though it was the most tumultuous period of the French Revolution. There had been years when it was unwise to praise a popular leader: today's member of the directorate was tomorrow morning's first visitor to the guillotine, "the razor that is only needed once."

Looking at the poverty around him only strengthened his belief in the present campaign. *Napoleon will lead us up*, he thought. *We will all be cared for.* But in that instant, his mind drifted to the face of Martin, frozen in his last gaze of agony and confusion. Others too: Rene, Jacques, and Daniel; all had died defending scows and barges from the English. All were left in shallow graves above that worthless, bloody harbor, their final resting places marked only with wooden crosses.

As he questioned the events of the last few days, he passed his own door three times, wandering the narrows of his neighborhood until someone caught him by the arm and spun him around, startling the horse.

"My boy, it's good to see you!" Louis Bossuet said, hugging him. "Just look at you. Quite the dashing chevalier!" The tall, thin man was always friendly to Albert and his grandmother, giving them money when he could spare it and affection constantly. "How is our army treating you?" Louis noticed tears in Albert's eyes. "What is wrong, boy?"

"It's nothing, Louis." Albert wiped away the tears

and with them the images of his dead friends. "How have you been?"

"I have never been better. The government recently purchased all the material I had in stock for uniforms, and I will not have to work another day this year! Though, I must say, all my work has been for line regiments—nothing that shines and sparkles as much as you!"

Louis was a tailor in the third arrondissement of Paris, though he usually only made clothes for local families there. Since the age of eleven, Albert had been his apprentice.

"That is indeed great news." Albert smiled and clapped him on the shoulder. They turned and walked together in the direction of Albert's house a few doors away.

"Have you been to see your grand-mère yet?" Louis asked.

"No, I was just touring the neighborhood. It feels as though I have been away a very long time. I half expected all the houses to be changed and I to be lost and wandering aimlessly, but now it seems I am what has changed."

Louis nodded with understanding. War always changed men; it was inescapable. Cheerfully he announced, "Well, come then. You will find her reassuringly unaltered. It is one of the things grand-mères do best! Besides, she will be relieved to know that you are alive."

The last words sank into Albert's heart and he pictured again all of those who would never return to their families.

Tethering the horse and entering the familiar home took Albert's mind off of war. The place smelled of cookfire smoke, very pleasant compared to the stink of cannons. Ever since Albert was small, Heloise never let the fire die, even in the hottest months. Hot food, she said, was the sovereign remedy for all sorts of ills.

A black iron kettle suspended over the coals produced a different kind of aroma. Albert inhaled deeply, and his mouth began to water. Heloise's onion soup was Albert's favorite dish, and he had longed for it daily since his departure for the army months before.

Louis closed the rickety door behind them. "She heard you might be coming. Everyone in the quarter knows what you did, and we're all very proud of you."

Albert just smiled sheepishly. "Nana?" he called. "Are you here?"

A voice pleasantly comforting to Albert sang back from behind a curtained doorway. "Albert! I knew it would be today, I'm so glad you're back." The curtain folded back and Heloise Penfeld emerged. She was plump and short, the exact opposite of Louis. Countless days of smiling, even through the hard times, had lined her face with a permanent fan of wrinkles around her eyes and mouth.

She rushed forward and embraced Albert, the curls of her gray hair dead level with his muscled chest. "I'm happy to be home," he said, kissing her forehead.

She stepped back and scanned his form from head to toe, looking past the uniform and seeing the young man. "You look too thin," she said. "I must fatten you up before you go back. Also let me see that arm." She led him to the simple plank table near the hearth. One table leg was too short, and the board rocked because of it. Albert was oddly pleased that no one had repaired it during his absence. Heloise clucked over the wounded arm, grudgingly admitted that it seemed to be healing well, poulticed it anew, and asserted, "And you look tired too. Have you slept, *mon petit* chevalier?" She coughed, wincing slightly.

The wafting aroma from the kettle made his stomach growl. "Not in two days," he said after swallowing back his hunger. "You are unwell?"

She waved away the question. "Goodness!" she exclaimed, coughing into her fist. "You must rest. Get right to bed."

"If you don't mind," Albert protested, "I'd rather eat first."

Louis broke silence to echo Albert's request with, "*Oui, oui,* madame!" and he drew himself up to the table as well.

"Not you, Louis," chided Heloise. "This entire kettle is for Albert."

Louis looked disappointed, thrusting out his lower lip in an exaggerated pout. Albert decided that though he could eat the whole cauldron of thick broth, he would save a bowl or two for his grand-mère's friend.

Heloise ladled the concoction into a carved wooden bowl and settled in beside Louis on the bench to watch him eat.

As Albert drank the soup down, he wondered idly if the two old friends would ever be married to each other. Except for Albert, they were both alone in the world, and Albert knew it would make his grand-mère very happy to have someone nearby now that he was away.

He finished the first bowl quickly, savoring the warming sensation it gave to his insides. Then, having satisfied the most severe of his hunger pains, he felt he could talk, and Heloise peppered him with questions about the war. Relating the story of his most recent battle with all due modesty brought disbelief as the couple were more likely to believe an embellished version of the truth. Albert did not oblige though, taking no pride in the actions that everyone else called heroic.

Speaking of the gunshot he had endured, Heloise scowled at the image of the enemy soldier responsible. She thumped the soup ladle against the cauldron with unnecessary force. When Albert related the cutlass blow, Heloise exclaimed and insisted on examining the wound.

At Albert's first yawn, Heloise led him to the straw-filled mattress in the small alcove where she slept.

"Sleep as long as you want, child," she whispered, as she covered him with a threadbare woolen blanket. "I'll be right here."

Albert listened as she said good-bye to Louis, and he fell asleep smiling when he heard the soft sound of a tender kiss the couple shared before parting.

When Albert lazily drifted back to consciousness, Heloise was sitting nearby. "How long have I been asleep?" he asked, stretching thoroughly.

"It is evening," Heloise said. "Would you like to eat again? I kept the soup warm."

He shook his head. "No, thank you." Sitting silent for a time as Heloise hummed, Albert thought of his life there. "Nana, tell me again about my mother."

"*Oui*, Albert," Heloise said, smiling gently. "Ariel

was a beautiful woman. Tall and fair, strong but loving. She used to say, 'One day I will have a crop of strong boys to care for us the rest of our days. They will be successful, they will live better lives than we have, they will make this country what it should be.'" Heloise pushed the dark locks of hair from his forehead, then mussed it up playfully. "You are fulfilling her wishes, Albert—making France the country it should be. Very admirable."

"Yes, Nana," he said, "but I killed men. There is nothing admirable in death." His gaze fell to the worn-out mattress under him.

"You are a soldier, and as such you fulfill your destiny as you do your duty. *Le bon Dieu* knows your heart and can see this as well."

Albert nodded and stood, pulling on his overshirt. "Thank you, Nana," he said. "You always help."

"Off to see Angelique?" she asked with a grin.

"Of course, where else would I go?" He strode past her, pausing to kiss her on the forehead. "I'll be back late. Sleep well."

When Albert Penfeld turned the corner of the Rue de la Huchette, immediately he caught a wave of such horrific odor that it struck him like a physical blow and turned his head.

Angelique's father was a drunkard, spending all his

money in dingy gambling halls and shady taverns. Were it not for those habits, Albert thought, they might move from this cesspit on the Left Bank of Paris. Had Angelique's mother still been alive, perhaps her father would not be so lost in his depression. He was a clochard; a perpetual drunkard, making just enough francs from his trade as a knifegrinder and locksmith to buy his next bottle of a certain thin, astringent wine of Anjou. He favored the vinegary fluid because it was cheap, plentiful, and easily consumed in quantities large enough to induce a continuous stupor. It took all of Angelique's meager earnings to supply the wilted cabbage and mildewed sausage on which they lived.

Rue de la Huchette was lined with large carriage portals leading to courtyards. These once stately homes were a legacy of some two hundred years earlier when the quarter had been a fashionable address. La Huchette's current status was more accurately portrayed by the stagnant sewage filling the central gutter of the uneven street. Originally designed to channel the mess into the Seine, the cobbles had settled over time, and the liquid pooled at the front stoops of some residences.

Angelique's home was one of those. Albert stepped carefully from island to island to avoid ruining his tall gleaming boots or splashing his uniform.

Gazing up at the facade of the building, he studied

the home in which Angelique resided. Two centuries of patched plaster and layers of peeling paint met his gaze, and it seemed no repairs had even been attempted in the last five decades. The right-hand gate of the once proud eight-foot-high carriage portal was missing, and the left side was permanently bent inward on a single rusted hinge. The walls inside the courtyard were streaked with green mold, orange rust, and black stains from the lead of the roof. The windows were boarded over after first being broken out.

It was not uncommon for more than one family to share a residence that had formerly belonged to a single well-off household. Such was the case at number five, where fifteen families were crammed into the space.

When Albert climbed three flights of dangerously swaying stairs and pounded on a rickety wooden door, an elderly man unknown to him answered it.

"*Oui?*" The man coughed, his tufted fringe of gray hair wafting in the putrid breeze.

"Angelique Chambord, s'*il vous plaît.*"

The man slammed the door in Albert's face, and the sound of his shuffling footsteps trailed away up the hall. A few moments later the door swung open again, but it was not Angelique. Instead, her father, Simon, glared down at Albert from the open passage. He was a large man, fat and dirty, wearing ragged, smelly clothes. His trousers were so shabby that only the coating of grease with which they were covered seemed to be holding them together. Even over the sewage-filled street, Albert could smell the man.

"Look at you!" Simon belched. "Dressed smart in the emperor's new clothes."

Albert knew Simon hated Napoleon and was trying to provoke him, but Albert was determined not to bicker with the man.

"And you look very well yourself, monsieur," Albert lied. Then he asked, "Is Angelique within?" He tried to look past the bulky man, but Simon moved in front of his gaze.

"Hear me, you imp in a monkey suit." Simon stepped forward. "That was no compliment. I knew that wretched little corporal, Bonaparte, when 'e lived a block from here. 'E was one of us then, poor and oppressed. 'Is 'ome was on the Street of the Fishing Cat, and many times 'e made supper of fish guts that not even the cats would drag home! Now look at 'im in 'is grand style, putting on airs! *Mordioux!* Napoleon is destroying this country, and you are helping! I'll be blasted if you'll lead my daughter to believing in that little..."

"Monsieur," Albert interrupted, "I cannot continue this conversation. You can be arrested for dissidence and treason. S'*il vous plaît*, think of your daughter. If you were arrested. . ."

Simon stepped forward and threw a fist at Albert's jaw. Albert was able to evade the blow enough to reduce the impact but still was sent sprawling to the ground. His shako rolled across the cobbles.

"Arrested?" Simon heaved a great laugh. "And who will come for me? You?" He laughed again and turned back inside, passing a crying Angelique as she hurried out.

His face throbbing with pain, Albert lay stunned, reclining on one elbow and glaring up at the door as Simon disappeared inside.

Angelique rushed to him.

Angelique and Albert strolled along the Seine as the Paris sun sank lower behind the skyline.

"I'm so sorry about that," Angelique whispered, turning to touch the knot forming above Albert's left eye. "I don't know what came over him."

"I understand your father's frustration," Albert said, staring into the red clouds that silhouetted the buildings. "But he is wrong about Napoleon. War is a great evil and yet the times now are not so evil as during the Reign of Terror a decade ago. This country is on the mend, and things will be better—he'll see."

They walked awhile in silence, enjoying the evening lull in the city's activity. Looming in the distance, the Notre Dame cathedral glowed orange in the dying light, the sunset beams playing about the spires and peaks of the flying buttresses, while much of the building was already in shadow. The whole effect was of an altar draped in sable and gold cloth, on top of which were a hundred blazing candles.

"Albert," Angelique said softly.

Hearing his name called so pleasantly electrified Albert; he temporarily forgot the pain over his eye. "Yes, love?"

"I worry about you."

"About me? What about me?"

"The war. . . I'm worried you won't be alive to see the changes you fight for. I. . ."

"Angelique, please." Albert cut her short. "What I'm doing is for the good of the people. Grand-mère says that in the tragedy of death. . ."

"I don't care what Heloise says, I want to know what Albert says!" A stamp of her foot and a toss of her hair underlined how earnest Angelique was. "There is nothing in the tragedy of death but death. So tell me as a person, not a patriot. Are you afraid of dying?"

The vehemence of her interrogation caught him off guard and he stopped walking, his jaw agape. "A-

Angelique," he stuttered, trying to demonstrate a certainty he did not himself fully feel, "I *am* a patriot."

"No, not to me! You are my love, my life." She stormed toward him with a pointed finger, backing him into the stone embankment below the Pont St. Michelle. "My only..." Her gray eyes sparked with blue flashes of emotion as she broke into tears.

"Oh, Angelique," Albert whispered, petting her soft hair as her tears soaked into his shoulder. "*Mon chérie*, I am not so afraid of dying," he said, looking up toward the great cathedral, "as I am of killing."

Angelique pushed away from his embrace and looked into his eyes. "I am not so afraid of dying as I am of living without you." Her delicate chin trembled, and she fought to keep her voice even. "And there are plenty of horrible people who won't be afraid of killing you!" Sobbing, she turned from him and walked toward the gargoyle faces that lined Pont Neuf.

Albert was awestruck. *How could I not see*, he thought, *how she worries for me?* He chased after her. "Angelique, wait." He caught her by the shoulder. "I will come back to you, I swear."

"How can you swear? Your promises to me mean nothing to the British."

"I know because God wills it. I am called to fight this war for us, so that *we* may have a future together. So the life I give you will be the best I can offer. This I can promise."

Angelique searched his face for any sign of doubt.

Albert wondered if his own fears were visible.

"Then marry me," she demanded abruptly.

"How?" he shot back without thinking. "Despite this fine new uniform, I have no money. We do not even have the five francs to stand before the registrar. How can I give you a church and a priest?" By the trembling of Angelique's lip, Albert knew she was again close to tears. He had sworn his love to her, but now at her first demand for proof he was hesitating. What must she think of him and his promises?

Her next words opened her heart to him. "I'll marry you with this beautiful sunset as a witness, here and now." Then gesturing toward the gleaming cathedral, she added, "And Our Lady of Paris knows I will be true to you. Could we afford to fill a church with flowers and candles, it would not shine as beautifully."

Taking a deep breath, Albert answered her spirit from his own. "And my witness shall be this river," he said, waving grandly up and down the Seine. "As its ribbon flows from far away even to the sea, still it is one river and unbroken. So shall my love be for you, even when we are far apart." Albert tilted his head back and rejoiced at the first sparkle that winked in the night sky.

"By God above, you *are* my wife, and when I come back again we will recite our vows in a church, and we will live long and happy together."

Angelique's gentle face shone in the twilight as the couple strolled on to the gardens of St. Julien le Pauvre.

It was not until sunrise that Albert delivered Angelique back to her door. They embraced on the stoop, sharing a lasting kiss that sent shivers down Albert's spine. "*Je t'aime*," he whispered. "I love you, Angelique, and I will return soon."

She squeezed him tighter. "Do you have to go?" She was already holding back tears. "Why will they not let you rest awhile?"

"They need me," Albert replied. "France needs me, and so it is for our own good that I must go."

The gelding neighed impatiently at the hitch where he had stood since the evening before.

"Coming," Albert quipped. "Please, Angelique, I must go." Kissing her one more time, he self-consciously straightened the folds of his pelisse cloak, mounted the large bay horse, and trotted away, watching her over his shoulder until he turned a corner.

He stopped briefly at Heloise's house to say good-bye. She was asleep, breathing lightly and peacefully, when he walked in. Placing a hand on her shoulder, he gently wakened her. "Good-bye, Nana," he said. "Stay well."

She rubbed her eyes and sat up quickly, "And you, Albert. Go with God. You are no help to me dead." She smiled, but her breathing roughened, and she coughed loudly and painfully.

"Get better, Nana," he whispered. "I need you."

She patted his head as he kissed her cheek. "Come home soon."

He strode from the house and set off for Boulogne.

During the tedious ride, he thought about the war. *Do I believe in it?* he wondered. *Am I doing right? Is there a God? If so, why does he allow so much suffering?* And then his thoughts flitted to himself. *If God is love, why must I be parted from those I love?*

Albert knew he was not brave that day; but he would continue acting brave because it was expected of him. Was that how everyone lived? *Everyone loves an image they have of me*, he mused. *But would anyone love me if they truly knew me?*

CHAPTER 5

———⟨✦⟩———

The voices of the choir soared out the doorway of St. John's church in Hampstead. Beneath the overhanging oaks that lined the flagstone walk the words were muffled, but then they emerged in full clarity to resonate past the wrought-iron fronted homes of Church Row. The congregation gathered to sing and pray for the safety of their men in battle and for the protection of the Almighty for the nation:

> *Oh God, our help in ages past,*
> *our hope for years to come,*
> *our shelter 'mid the stormy blast*
> *and our eternal home!*

The words called out to all the troubled, frightened hearts, in phrases convicting and forgiving, cleansing and uplifting.

Inside the two-hundred-year-old stone church, the experience was even more poignant. "Brothers and sisters, pray that our sacrifice will be acceptable to God," the white-haired Anglican priest intoned.

Kneeling, the congregation responded, "Lord, I am not worthy to receive you. But only say the word and I shall be healed."

As the invitation to receive the Eucharist was given, Randolph Sutton stood and opened the gate in the Sutton family pew. He tenderly escorted William's mother, Julia, to the altar. Ever since the deaths of her husband, Bryce, and son Charles, twenty-some years before, Julia Howard Sutton had been frail and often ill. Even so, in the shimmering waves of color cast by the light streaming through the stained glass windows, she had a fine, almost translucent beauty.

Brightly clothed, William wore a pea-green velvet coat with tails and dark burgundy breeches. But there was no color in his countenance. His face had a diluted, leaden appearance, and his eyes were tired and lifeless.

Slouching in his seat, William was dubious he would ever be able to get up from the pew. Sighing deeply, William made his way out to the aisle, tagging lazily behind. With heavy steps, he trod carelessly on the peacefulness and sanctity of the church. He stopped at the altar only momentarily to glance at the wooden crucifix on the wall behind the priest before kneeling down at a wooden rail with the others.

The priest held aloft a morsel of bread and recited, "The body of Christ," before offering it to Julia.

Even though it would soon be William's turn to receive, his thoughts were far from the sacrifice of Christ or William's own need for repentance. Instead he was staring down the row of kneeling parishioners at a pair of shabbily dressed servants: someone's maid and stable-hand, no doubt.

The ragged-looking man with sunken eyes, a stubble of whiskers, and dry, cracked lips, leaned over the rail in silent prayer, tears streaming down his lined cheeks. The priest placed a single piece of bread on the man's lips. Beside the man was an equally shabby woman. She too was given a portion of bread.

William watched as the priest placed the fragment into the woman's almost toothless mouth. It disgusted him. How could they let these lowborn folk in at the same time as the gentry? He rolled his eyes impatiently, waiting for his turn. When it came he chewed the morsel without tasting and swallowed without thinking.

A second priest passed along the rail with a silver chalice. "The blood of Christ," he offered. He lifted the cup to the lips of the ragged man. With closed eyes the man leaned his head back, accepting the gift.

In his mind, William condemned the frayed pair yet again, silently accusing them of coming in for the sake of the wine. He sneered, imagining the couple frequenting every communion service of the day.

The priest lowered the cup, held a cloth to the rim, then presented the chalice to the woman. William watched as she smiled through tears at the priest, mouthing the words, *thank you.*

Moving on to Lord Sutton and Julia, they also completed the holy rite, before the servant of God came to William. He fought back thoughts of the servant woman and her dreadful, toothless mouth touching the side of the cup, her scruffy husband craving every last drop of the liquor. All of these images made him cringe and tense as the priest held the cup to his mouth. He pulled his head back, trying to avoid taking any of the liquid.

Realizing only the difficulty of William's awkward position, the priest tipped the cup higher, dumping a mouthful in. William flinched forward, clanking a tooth on the hard rim of the cup. He opened his eyes and glared at the priest.

The Suttons and the rest returned to their seats.

Just before the benediction, the older priest interrupted the service to make a special announcement. He called for the ragged couple, seated at the extreme rear of the nave, to stand , which they reluctantly did.

"I know you will want to join me," the priest suggested, "in remembering in prayer our dear brother and sister, Hugh and Katie O'Donnell. It was just yesterday that they received word of their son, Frank, killed in Spain while fighting against the French."

William opened the carriage door painted with the anchor and mermaid arms of the House of Sutton and climbed in, scooting to the far side. Lord Randolph helped Julia up. She reached out to William for assistance, but he was looking away across the heath and the endless stretch of green pasture. Grassy knoll succeeded tufted hillock all the way to where he could see the dome of St. Paul's gleaming in the sunlight.

"William!" Lord Sutton snapped. "Your mother is ill. Give her your hand!"

William pursed his lips and wrinkled his brow. "Sorry, Mother. I did not realize."

"No matter," she said softly, pulling up the hem of a pale-blue satin dress before seating herself on the opposite side of the carriage, facing the rear. "Off in a world somewhere else?"

"Yes," William said, "galloping out over the heath on a great white stallion."

The image made her smile.

Julia's entire frail existence was wrapped up in the life of her son. If he had not existed, she would have ceased to live many years before. She was kind, giving, and tenderhearted, and sought to fulfill William's every request, though he himself offered nothing in return beyond small talk and an occasional kiss on the cheek. She saw him as if he were still an innocent child, and it warmed her heart. For William, on the other hand, her perspective was nothing more than an effective means to control his mother and through her, his grandfather.

"Driver! Away," Lord Sutton instructed, climbing into the carriage. The ride was already under way by the time he had slammed the door. "William! Show some courtesy!"

Julia held up her hand to stop his words. "Really, it was nothing. There is enough unhappiness in the world already. Think of the poor O'Donnells."

William turned to watch the passing scenery. Lord Sutton sat cross-armed, frowning, while Julia clung to a leather strap and closed her eyes.

Lord Sutton knew the way William operated his mother, but he possessed an unquestioning love for his daughter-in-law, a love that knew no wrongs. Fearful of making her intense sorrows worse, Lord Sutton was careful to avoid speaking out too harshly against William while in her presence.

Eager to look good in front of his mother, William at last opened a conversation in a jolly tone. "I spoke to the sailmaker last night."

"Last night?" Grandfather Sutton questioned. "And where were you to speak to such a fellow last night?"

"It is of little importance where, since the good news that followed is what counts."

"So out with it then."

Julia opened her eyes. "Father, is there really a need to be so abrupt?"

William acted momentarily as if he were hurt by Lord Sutton's words, then continued, "He's one of Thomas's friends."

"Thomas!" Julia interjected. "How is he?"

"Oh, he's splendid. Just got a commission in the Royal Marines."

"How lovely. From the time you were little and played together, I knew you boys would succeed."

Lord Sutton interrupted. "Yes, well it's a shame they all haven't." He said this while looking directly at William.

Julia closed her eyes and withdrew once more.

"Anyway, he says he has a friend whom he thinks can help us with the sails."

"Is he reputable?"

"Quite. His name is John Anson. He retired several years ago after a glorious career on the HMS *Invincible*—even took part in the battle of the Glorious First of June!"

"Well done, then. And he must be a lucky man too, to survive the wreck at Great Yarmouth."

"I'd agree. Captain Rennie and over four hundred men were dragged down with her that day off Harborough Sands."

"And what sort of price break can he give us?"

"Unfortunately, none. I'm sure every sailmaker these days has doubled their price."

"Then I fail to see how this is of any help to us at all," Lord Randolph grumped.

Pitching his voice to show his long-suffering patience, William said, "It is mainly because he has the fabric and can begin measurements at once. He must be the only sailmaker who's not completely booked."

Under the inquiring gaze of his daughter-in-law's now wide-open blue eyes, Lord Sutton offered grudging approval of William's initiative. "Well done. But you must personally go to Greenwich tomorrow and engage him."

This was exactly the sort of suggestion for which William was looking. He could pick up Judy on the way.

But he must not show his eagerness, or his grandfather would be suspicious. "Tomorrow? I've done so much dashing around lately I thought I would rest."

"Nonsense! Well begun is half done, but see the matter through, boy! Finish the job. If the man can begin at once, then you shall have to be there with him to take charge. And while there you can examine the steps of the fore, main, and mizzenmasts to see if they're in need of fresh tarring."

"But what about the money?"

"I'll send a banknote with you. You can take it to Telson's London branch on your way."

Grandfather Sutton pulled out a leather pocketbook from his coat and began writing. He signed his name, folded the sheet, and handed it to William.

William opened the note. "I'm afraid this won't be enough."

"Well, how much should it be?" Lord Sutton demanded. "One thousand?"

"I'm just thinking that if the steps and mains need resealing then there is no sense in leaving the toppers to rot. So maybe we should do all of them since the rigging is going to be inspected anyway."

Surprised to find William in the least knowledgeable and even more startled to note actual interest in business matters, Lord Sutton said, "Good thinking, lad. How much then?"

"Three hundred pounds should be sufficient." William had already calculated a sum that would replace the lost wager and still be sufficient for the actual ship-repair needs.

"My boy, you must think that I am made of money."

William shrugged. "It is the price we pay for getting attention to our needs. But how much will be lost in cargo revenues if *Stronghold* does not sail on time?"

"Give me that back." Lord Sutton mumbled under his breath as he tore up the old bank draft and wrote a new one. "Here. Give this to Mr. Shaw of Telson's, and he shall see you on your way with a carriage and strong-box."

"Mr. Shaw would be terrible unhappy wif us if he knew we was doin' this. We is goin' exactly opposite to Greenwich," protested the driver of the coach belonging to Telson's Bank.

"Don't be an impertinent twit. You know what a prime client Sutton and Company is to the bank. If we had asked Mr. Shaw he'd have gladly done the same. In fact, he would have insisted that you follow my instructions." William spoke to the driver of the Telson coach through a small window positioned so that the passenger was looking between the ankles of the coachman. Though narrow, over the driver's footrest one had quite a view of whatever was directly in front of the carriage, but this dry summer afternoon mostly what one saw was dust and bugs. "I appreciate this greatly, and I promise you'll be well taken care of for it."

William was startled by an upside-down grinning face that poked into the rectangular hole. "And I suppose you is goin' to fund me pension if you is wrong?"

William barked, "Don't worry so much!" He shoved the man away by his ample nose and closed the slider. William believed that the sudden attack of professional anxiety by the driver was merely a ploy to get him to increase the size of the bribe. Still, it would be best if no one besides the driver ever knew of this little detour. Settling back in the burgundy leather seat, William looked out the window just as the coach slowed to climb the steepest part of Hampstead High Street and rounded a bend. There, beside the coach road was the white stone marker that gave its name to White Stone Pond. The Telson coach clattered down the cobbled ramp into the pool, cooling and wetting the wheels and spokes and allowing the draft horses to drink.

Without reopening the window the driver called, "Jack Straw's Castle dead ahead."

The driver clucked to the horses who walked up the

other ramp and out of the pond. As soon as they were clear of the water, William shouted, "Let me off here, then park out of sight around back." He hopped out of the coach a hundred yards from the tavern, which was built to imitate a fourteenth-century castle. The resemblance was not very convincing at midday.

Inside Jack Straw's Castle Pub, William searched through the crowded mob for Judy. All there seemed to be enjoying a plowman's lunch and a pint of bitter. It was food for the lower classes, but William would admit that there were days when a chunk of Stilton, a hunk of heavy brown bread, and a pint of bitter just could not be beaten.

"Have you seen Judy?" he questioned a plump barmaid who was pulling pints.

She looked at him cautiously and scratched her nose with her wrist behind three foaming pints. "What do ye wont with 'er?"

"I'm going to wrap her in my arms and kiss her." The woman's eyes lit up. "I'm going to lift her out of this life and carry her into the heavens, where I shall smother her with kisses."

The barkeeper nodded knowingly and said drily, "Then ye must be the angel wot she's been tellin' me about."

Judy walked around the corner with a wooden tray

full of empty cups perched high above her head. "William! How lovely to see you. What are you doing here?"

"I'm here to take you to see a ship. My ship."

"Now?" She set the tray down, brushed off her hands, and looked at her spattered apron. "But I'm working."

"Not to worry. I'll square it with your employer."

"But I'm in my dingies."

"No matter," he reassured her, kissing her hand. "Some sailors wear even less. Now, who's in charge?"

Judy looked at the woman behind the bar.

"It's me, yer lordship, Beth Foster, at yer service."

"Wonderful," William said, laughing and not at all dismayed. "Beth, you wouldn't mind if I take Judy away for a short holiday? I promise to return her tomorrow."

"Only if ye take me as well. As chaperon, doncha see?" She wiped her glistening face on a bar towel and made as if to untie her apron.

Quickly dabbing his own forehead, William searched for an excuse. "But you, dear lady, would be too much of a distraction for my poor senses."

The woman blushed, then giggled and began to laugh. "Just ye be watchin' this'un, Judy," she warned. "He's a smooth'un, 'e is."

"Tell you what, Beth. Since I know you will have

Judy's work to do as well as your own, let me reward you for letting her go." He reached deep into his pocket. "Here you are, my good woman." Smiling he set half a crown on the counter in front of her.

"But what about my gratuity?" The sweaty woman leaned toward him with lips puckered.

William's eyes grew as big as a rabbit's that was about to be eaten by a hawk. Judy grabbed his wrist. He could see the excitement on her face. She nudged him to go on and kiss Beth.

"Come on then! Where's my kiss?"

"One does not lightly profane such a holy shrine," William said with reverence. "Close your eyes again."

The woman snapped her lids shut and waited.

Tugging at Judy's arm, William motioned for her to sneak out. Her shoulders shaking with suppressed laughter, she quickly removed her apron and set it on the counter.

"Don't peek now," William warned. "You'll ruin the surprise." Hurrying to Horace, the biggest, hairiest plowman in the pub, William pulled at him to come over. The man bobbed his head with an openmouthed smile. William leaned close to the woman and spoke softly. "Here it is. . . ."

Then the troll-like plowman grabbed the woman with two hands behind her head and squeezed his drooping mustaches against her mouth. William was reminded of an apple being eaten by a horse.

When Beth saw who it was, she attempted to scream. But all that came out was something that sounded like a muffled belch. The entire pub roared with laughter as she flogged Horace away from her, chasing him around the counter, as William and Judy ran away hand in hand to the waiting coach.

Below London Bridge was the anchorage of the Pool of London, the farthest upriver that oceangoing ships could travel. Downstream from the port, the river Thames wandered eastward, passing the Isle of Dogs. Both up- and downstream it was surrounded by ship-yards, warehouses, and docks for goods arriving from all over the world. On the south-side of the river was Greenwich, home to the Royal Naval Hospital and the Naval College. A three-masted ship-of-the-line, carrying seventy-four guns and with all thirty sails hanging loose to dry, gleamed in the afternoon sunlight as she swung at anchor in the stream.

Telson's carriage deposited William and Judy in front of Helmsteder's Chandlery. William left the young woman to admire the activity along the river while he entered the shop.

The persuasion of the gold coins in the heavy chest

soon convinced Helmsteder to agree to all of William's requirements for refitting the *Stronghold*. New sails, tarring, and rigging were soon all contracted for, as were the services of John Anson as rigger. Both the time of delivery and the amount of payment required allowed William to redeem his earlier errors with no one the wiser.

He returned to the river's edge to find Judy in rapt admiration of the seventy-four. Then he noted that she was coyly waving toward the officer of the deck of the warship. He cleared his throat roughly to make her turn around.

"Where is our carriage going?" she asked, watching Telson's coach pull out of the drive and head up the London road.

"To arrange some things for me while we walk over and take a look at my ship." William cocked his head, urging her to walk along. "It will only take a few minutes."

"Oh, no need to hurry on my account," she said, peering out from under the wide brim of her straw hat. "I could spend as much time as you like here."

Knowing his special plans, William held back a smile, never letting on. They strolled quickly down a long wharf by a warehouse where a dozen docks jutted out perpendicular to the shore. They turned down the third one, and tied up fast on the right side was a two-masted ship. Unlike the first-rate man-of-war, its top deck was not very high above the dock. There was not even a gangway to board the vessel, only a rope ladder.

William ushered Judy to the ladder. She paused, leaning over the edge of the dock to look down at the gap between her and the ship.

"Don't think about that," William said, stepping up close behind her. Placing his hands on her hips he continued, "It's always best not to look down until you know what you're doing."

Grabbing the ropes without a backward glance, Judy began climbing. When she was five steps up, she turned to face him and said confidently, "Oh, I'm not afraid of heights."

At first her bravery put William off. He was trying to be chivalrous, and she made him feel that it was unnecessary. "I know, but the water is really murky. Who knows what creature is lurking beneath us, having followed the ship in from sea?" At that she squeaked and scurried faster, not objecting to the pat he gave her leg every other step.

"So here we are on the main deck," William said, hopping over the rail and lifting Judy down with two hands on her waist. "Welcome to the *Stronghold*. May I take the liberty of escorting you around?"

She smiled and nodded.

"That is the foremast," he said, pointing as he walked up the deck cluttered with piles of rigging and heaps of tattered sailcloth. "And back there is the mainmast."

"This ship is quite a bit smaller than the other one we saw."

"Indeed."

"Is this a warship?"

"No." William turned. "No. This is a light cargo ship."

Judy looked dissatisfied.

"If it were a naval ship, it would be called a sloop. Probably the biggest guns it would have would be eight pounders. And even at that weight, probably only four of them." He held up his hand to show her the size of ball a four pounder would fire. "About the size of a small apple."

She did not seem impressed. "Well, what could that do against a great big vessel like the first one I saw?"

William sighed. "To be honest, in a straightforward battle, not a lot." He could not tell if she was frankly curious or just trying to provoke him. "But I've heard stories of small ships taking larger ones. If one doesn't have size to rely on, then one must have cunning wit to compensate. It's all in the tactics, you see."

"Oh, I see," Judy answered drily.

William imagined she was probably thinking of the naval officer who had so easily captured her attention. He and his first-rate could go to Davy Jones for all William cared. He gritted his teeth. His annoyance made him want to punish her, so he said, "Anyway, do you know what a four-pound chunk of iron would do to a skull?"

She waited.

"Part your pretty red strands, my dear." He coldly outstretched his hand toward her face. He began to brood over the fact that his plans were not working out and that jealousy was making him say stupid things.

Judy changed the subject with a kiss. "Show me the rest of the ship, Captain."

"Right this way, my lady," he agreed.

William led her toward the stern and up a short flight of steps to the poop deck. At the top he turned to her and bowed, then directed her attention to a lantern on a cloth-covered table beside the taffrail.

"Oh, William!" she exclaimed. Judy hurried over to the table, elegantly set for two to dine. "How wonderful!" She spun round and locked her mouth on his for several seconds.

Oh what she does to me, he thought. "I knew you would enjoy it." He lifted a silver serving lid, revealing a roast duck. Two more dishes were uncovered, displaying a tureen of potatoes, peas, and cabbage, and a loaf of freshly baked bread.

"Let me help you," he said, pulling up a chair for Judy as she sat down. He joined her, and they watched the sun set while enjoying their meal.

The last rays trickled off the water as the sky turned a brilliant pink, fading toward them in deepening color.

They talked a little about the war and the threatened invasion, a little about Old Boney, and then William told her more about sailing and life at sea. Mostly, though, as William noted, Judy could not keep her eyes off him. Before they realized it, supper was through, the sunset was gone, and now the only light was that from the lantern. It cast a warm seductive glow on Judy's eyes.

"And for dessert. . ." William lifted the lid of the last covered serving tray. "Strawberry tarts."

"Mmm, my favorite," she replied. "Well, my second favorite."

William looked surprised. How could he have guessed wrong? "And what would be your first?"

She grinned, grabbing hold of his lapels. "You," she said, leaning in to give him another of her dizzying kisses.

"Perhaps you would like a walk before dessert," he offered clumsily, having difficulty speaking. "I could show you around the other decks."

"I'd love to," she concluded.

Without another word he led her below, leaving dessert for later.

William lit a lantern in the companionway. "These are the captain's quarters," he said, thrusting open a louvered door.

It was not very large for a captain's room. Cluttered with stacks of maps and navigational equipment, it was close and sparsely furnished, apart from desk, chair, and bunk.

Beside a set of leaded glass windows that spanned the beam of the stern, William embraced her. They held each other for a moment, then William began to edge her toward the captain's bunk. Suddenly he noticed something peculiar outside.

It was a strange orange glow, reflecting off the sails of the ship next to the sloop in the adjacent dock. The light wavered and seemed to be growing brighter. Soon he smelled smoke. An agonizing wave of dread washed over him. At that moment he realized there was a fire on board the ship.

"The lantern!" he shouted, jumping from the bed. There was a loud crash on the deck outside the captain's door. William ran to it in panic. It would not open. Shouldering into it hard, William was bounced backward off his feet. He stared at it for a moment as a tendril of black smoke curled under it.

Judy rushed to his side. "What are we to do?"

William thought quickly, looking around the room for a way out. *Windows*, he thought. But if they were to jump into the water, there would be no time left to try and put the fire out. Yet there would be no time left if he did not think of something fast. He charged over to the portside window. Opening it he leaned out and looked down at the water, where the flames now cast an evil glow. An ominous roaring had replaced the earlier crackling noises as the fire spread and took hold of the ship's timbers.

"Judy!" he ordered, scooping her up and carrying her toward the open port. "Jump and swim under the dock to safety." He pushed her toward the sill.

"Wait!" She shook loose his grip. "What about you?"

"I've got to go up there and see what I can do to save the ship. There's a ladder at the end of the dock. Swim toward it, and try to find help."

Judy let her legs dangle only an instant before she closed her eyes and pushed off. A second later she hit the water and began swimming before she even surfaced. William watched until she reached the ladder, then climbed out the window and up the curving stern of the ship.

Standing with his feet on the window ledge, William reached for the railing to pull himself up.

What greeted his eyes was an inferno past extinguishing. Empty barrels gushed flames like the mouths of furnaces. Heaps of sails and discarded rigging shot flares twenty feet and more into the ratlines and stays. Looming overhead, the masts, like giant torches, scorched his hair. Already the hull itself was being licked by flames. The lantern must have been knocked over somehow; but how could all this destruction have swelled so quickly?

There was barely a chance for William to save himself. Forward was no good; only a small gap in the flames toward the starboard rail beckoned him to safety.

Swaddling his face and head in his coat, he scurried underneath the flaming spanker sail. Just as he was about to leap overboard, he heard lines snapping and looked up to see the boom collapsing toward him. He leaped for the rail, but the falling timber caught him across the shoulders and knocked him to the deck.

His hands in the flames, William screamed and tore at the fiery beam that pinned him down. As he managed to push it aside, he scrambled to his feet again. His jacket was smoldering. The smoke and hot air were burning his lungs, his back, and blistering his neck. He screamed again, swatting at his head and smelling the stench of his singed hair.

With a last wave of energy, William flung himself toward the rail and dived over the side of the burning vessel.

Even down in the water William could feel the heat of the flames as they crackled and consumed the foremast. He swam hard toward the ladder and climbing up it, looked for Judy at the top. A knot of men with axes gathered beside the burning sloop's dock lines. He ran to them.

"Help me! Please, help me," a black-faced William pleaded with the men. "I have to put out this fire!"

One of the men shook his head furiously. "Too bad, mate, she's gone."

"NO!" William argued.

"Yes!" was the vehement reply. "We've got to cut her adrift before the entire dockyard goes up!" The figures returned to chopping through the lines.

William attempted to wrest the ax away from the man. Then as the lines parted and *Stronghold* drifted free, he lunged toward the cable end. The drag of the ship was pulling William toward the river when something slammed down on his head and he fell to the deck. The last thing he saw was the sloop entirely engulfed in flames.

When William awoke, the scene was no longer lit by amber flames but with the silvery glow of moonlight. With the rush of agony in his fingers and skull, he suddenly remembered what had happened. He sat up, almost blacking out again from the pain, then slowly opening his eyes to the sheen on the water. There, run hard aground on the far shore of the Thames, was the silhouette of the burned-out shell of the sunken sloop. He felt a pain in his chest, and tears started in his eyes. "Oh no!" he sobbed. "What have I done?"

Judy was standing in the middle of a ring of lantern-bearing onlookers, commenting on the wreckage, when she heard William's cry and ran to him.

How will I ever explain this? William wondered. There was no lie in the world that could save him this time.

She knelt to comfort him, but he pulled away, giving no thought to who had bandaged his hands or smeared the foul-smelling but healing ointment on his burns. "Leave me alone, you tart!" he shrieked, striking her face.

Tears started down her cheeks as he staggered to his feet. "But, William..." Unable to speak, she began to cry.

William's smoke-reddened eyes burned with hatred.

"None of this would have happened if it weren't for you!" he shouted. He staggered off in the darkness, raving, leaving Judy alone on the dock.

Half lame and nearly sightless from exhaustion, William staggered up the brick walkway of the Sutton estate. His clothes were in a ragged state, blackened with soot and shredded by some means he could not even remember.

Over and over his mind proposed the same question: *How am I going to break this news to my grandfather?* No answer came.

He felt the urge to cry. He winced and snarled, but no more tears would flow. *Grandfather might have me flogged ... or hanged. I don't know what he'll do. The only certain thing is that there is no way I could make this any worse than it is.*

"Oh, Lord!" he groaned aloud. "What on earth shall I do?" William collapsed near the front stoop, moaning in pain when the rocks lining the herbaceous border ground against his swollen, blistered hands. Again he begged, "God, what am I to do?"

He heard nothing but a lonely sighing wind and the constant ringing in his ears that resounded of breaking timbers and crackling fire. A vision of the sloop engulfed in flames tormented him. When he could not make it leave, his head began to spin.

William let out an agonizing scream as his head fell back on the steps, and then the house, silent a moment earlier, was alive with activity. One of the servants had heard his outcry and opened the door to find him there on the steps.

"Master William!" Samuel, the steward, responded in horror. Not knowing if William would die on the spot the man called for others to help him. He attempted to scoop William's limp body up into his arms.

As if from far away, William heard a voice calling, "Send for the doctor quickly, or he will surely die!"

William's mother heard the desperate calls of the steward and hurried to the door. "What is it?" she pleaded. A pair of housemaids tried to block her view, but craning her neck, she peered around them at the body.

"No, madame!" Samuel insisted. "Stay back. You mustn't see the state of your son!"

Julia forced her way past those who tried to restrain her and gasped aloud. Her blue-veined hand flew to her mouth as her skin whitened yet another shade paler than her usual milky complexion, and she collapsed on the ground beside William.

CHAPTER 6

Soon after his induction into the First Hussars, Cyrus affected a rolling gait that he proclaimed to be a swagger. Tiny wisps of his blond hair hung down before his ears and at the nape of his neck, in conscious imitation of the elaborate braided queues many cavalrymen sported. He sneered at the uniform belonging to any other branch of the service; for other hussar regiments he adopted a cold, thin smile and a brief nod. As he said, "Hussars are all better than all other soldiers, but only the First is ... the First!"

Albert could not help but laugh at his friend. If there was any truth in the old saying about clothes making the man, then it was amply demonstrated in Cyrus.

Not that they were full-fledged troopers, by no means. Neither Albert nor Cyrus had much previous experience with horses, so every day they rode thick-legged, broad-necked, simpleminded plugs until the men walked bowlegged and sat down gingerly, if at all.

To this enforced intimacy with equines was added musket drill, saber drill, and the necessity of learning myriad trumpet calls with which orders for complicated cavalry troop movements were dispatched on the battlefield. With a circle of raw recruits around him on the parade ground, Trumpeter LeClerc blew a series of fast, ascending notes and then waited expectantly for the response.

"Bivouac?" Cyrus ventured.

"Charge?" offered another trainee.

"*Sacré bleu!*" retorted LeClerc, wiping his brow with a pocket handkerchief. He looked at his instrument suspiciously as if it had mispronounced the notes. "How can you miss that one?" he pleaded. "It is the same as yesterday and the day before and the day before! It is. . ."

"Assembly," Albert suggested.

"*Certainement!*" agreed LeClerc. "What is wrong with the rest of you imbeciles? Do you have horse dung between your ears?" He noted Lieutenant Dupre waving from the sidelines and holding aloft a leather pouch. "Just so." He nodded. "Try this one," he said, and the trumpet warbled again.

"Mail call!" all the recruits responded.

"You *would* know that one," LeClerc grudgingly admitted. "Very well, dismissed."

Albert hung back from the crowd of men. He had received a letter from Angelique only two days earlier and so was not expecting anything from her. Heloise had never learned to write more than her name and so was confined to scrawling, "*Votre Nana*," at the bottom of Angelique's notes.

To Albert's surprise, his was one of the first names called. The folded paper was fine stock, sealed with red wax bearing the impression of a thimble. Albert knew it at once to be from Louis, his master in the tailor's guild and Nana's friend. Though never spoken of openly, Louis was believed to have aristocratic origins, hidden since the time of the Revolution, but still discernible in such things as stationery and sealing wax.

"My dear boy," Albert read. "I know that what I am about to relate will be difficult for you to hear. Your nana is gravely ill, dying. She has hidden this sad truth from Angelique and only recently has permitted me to speak of it to you. She is asking for you, Albert. She says she must relate something to you of great importance. What this matter is she will not say. It may be impossible for you to come at once. Nevertheless, if you do not arrive soon, I fear it will be too late. Your affectionate, Louis."

Albert read the letter through twice, unable to

comprehend its meaning on only one trial. When its import sank in, he bolted for the gate.

"Trooper Penfeld," Lieutenant Dupre bellowed. "Mounted drill in five minutes."

Albert did not reply. He knew the consequences of what he was doing, but nothing was going to stop him. Running into the stables, he asked the groom for the fastest mount available.

"That would be Balthasar there," the slow-witted stablehand remarked, indicating a buckskin stallion already saddled and bridled. "But you can't. . ."

Albert never heard the conclusion to the sentence, since he had already vaulted into the saddle and was on his way toward Paris.

Albert's face was ashen as he strode through the door and removed his battered shako. The plume was missing, and the lozenge plate bearing the emblem of the First Hussars was askew, but Albert took no notice.

All was silent in Heloise's dimly lit shanty except for the crackle of a fire in the small hearth that filled the rooms with smoke. Louis rose from a chair placed close to the glowing embers.

"Albert," he whispered, "thank God you've come. She asks for you constantly."

Grimacing and shrugging the pelisse off his shoulder, Albert said, "I came as soon as I could. Where is she?"

"She is asleep at present. Please, come sit by the fire and talk with me."

As they moved toward the fire, Albert could hear Heloise's labored breathing from behind the faded cloth partition that served as the door to her room. It pained him to know she was so near the end of her life.

"Sit boy, tell me about things in our emperor's forces."

"Louis, please." Albert only shook his head. He could think of nothing but his dying grandmother.

It should come as no shock, he thought, *she was always sick. But I also thought she would go on forever.*

As if reading Albert's mind, Louis said, "The way she struggled for breath of late—even coughing blood, though she tried to hide it from me, I knew she could not go on. But her pain will soon be no more. Isaiah 57 verse 2 says. . ."

"Louis!" Albert shouted. "Not now. Can you not see that I'm. . ." A noise beyond the curtain caught his attention, and he fell silent.

After a loud fit of wheezing, Heloise called to him in a voice that moved him to tears. "Albert? Could that be my Albert?"

"I am here, Nana. I am here." He eased back the

curtain and walked into the chamber where Heloise lay on linen-covered straw with her head propped up slightly.

How thin she is, Albert thought as he noticed how her cheekbones pressed against her skin and how like sticks her forearms were. *My nana was plump. I hardly know this woman.*

Heloise must have seen the look on his face for she said, "Only slimming down for the journey." She drew in a gravely breath. "*Mon petit agneau.*"

Little Lamb. Heloise had not called him that since he was twelve when he fought off two thieves and kept them from taking some groceries she had purchased. His hand unconsciously traced the outline of the three-inch scar at his hairline, a wound received in that very struggle. Nana had called it his "badge of honor."

Albert fingered the silver buttons of his dolman jacket and shifted his feet. "Do not talk this way, Nana. You will be fine."

She gave a little laugh that sounded to Albert like a spade scratching dry earth. Her face became serious. "Albert, I want to rest."

"Yes, Nana, and I'll be out here."

"No." Heloise made an effort to sit up but was seized with a spasm of hacking and slumped back to the bedding. "Before I can rest I must tell you a story."

Albert was confused but just nodded and sat next to her.

Heloise wheezed in another lungful of the dingy air. "When I was younger, I used to know a man named Francois D'Chiminee. He was a smuggler, but he had a good heart."

"Nana, I am no priest."

"Do not interrupt me." She coughed roughly, panting afterward. "I do not have time or breath. Please listen only." She composed herself and began again. "He was a smuggler living on a ship in Brest close to a quarter of a century ago. I lived in that town as well; it was where I was raised."

Now Albert started. He wanted to question her, for all his life she had told him she was from St. Malo, many miles to the east of Brest.

Heloise saw the look in his eyes. Slowly she apportioned enough breath for the words, "I am from Brest. One day he came to me with a package that he said he had found. He could not tell me where; he only said he should not have been there. He asked me to care for it, that it was very precious, but nothing for which he could accept the responsibility . . . a child." She sat silent for a moment, looking up at his face.

Albert was perplexed. "He found a child? This man just *found* a. . ." Slowly his lips parted as his jaw fell.

Heloise reached for him, touching the tips of her fingers to the scar, and he pulled away. "*Agneau.*"

Albert's eyes grew wide in disbelief. "But you and my . . . ma mère," he said, tears welling up in his eyes. "You have told me so many times of my mother. What she was like, what she said."

"Albert, there was nothing else I could do." Heloise's outstretched arm waved in the air in a feeble gesture of futility and fell back to her side. "I wanted you to look upon a broader world than a Breton fisherman sees."

"My name." He rubbed his forehead again. "My family."

"Albert, *agneau.*"

"No! I am not." He sobbed. "Why did you not tell me?" Tears streamed from under his palms as he pressed them into his eyes. "Why?" Anger grew in his chest, and his heart beat faster. "Why?" Sound faded from his ears, and he clenched his eyes more tightly.

"*Je t'aime, agneau,*" Heloise whispered, then fell silent.

Albert caught his breath and looked up, wiping tears away. "Nana?" He took her frail hand in his. "Grand-mère?" Her breath came only in gasps, and he patted her hand. "Nana!"

He began to sob, released her hand, and backed from

her, nearly falling through the curtain. Turning from the room, he came face-to-face with Angelique.

Her face echoed the pain she felt for him. "Albert?" She raised a hand to his cheek, but he turned away. "Albert," she repeated, "I heard. I know. I'm so sorry."

"No!" he yelled, looking away. Charging past her for the door, he shouted, "I am not Albert! I don't even know who I am!"

Upon his return to camp in Boulogne two days later, Albert was arrested. He said such treatment was agreeable to him; he was going to give himself up anyway. Since the preparations for the invasion of England had been under way at the time he decamped, he could have been charged with desertion. Such a crime, if a guilty verdict resulted from the court-martial, would end in Albert facing a firing squad.

Instead, Lieutenant Dupre took the melancholy young man aside and listened to what he had to say. While not fully comprehending all that Albert struggled to relate about his past and his lack of identity, Dupre recognized qualities of manhood too valuable to destroy.

Moreover, much change was happening in camp. It was rumored that there was trouble on the eastern front and that the army would sooner be fighting Russians and Austrians than the British.

After a conference with Captain Limoges and Colonel Rouvillois, it was decided that Albert would be charged with "unauthorized use of a cavalry mount," and "failure to report for drill as ordered."

Albert pleaded guilty.

The sentence was twelve lashes.

The ranks of the First Hussars were drawn up in a tight square around the scene of the punishment. It was tacitly agreed that while chastisement was necessary, there was still no reason to open regimental discipline to the gaze of outsiders.

Stretched over the spare wheel on the back of a company supply wagon, Albert's dolman was stripped off, exposing his bare back. At a painfully slow, measured pace, the sergeant-at-arms swung the heavy cat against Albert's skin as Lieutenant Dupre kept the count. At the third swing Albert's shoulders were crisscrossed with welts; by the sixth they ran with blood.

When the punishment had been completed and the regiment dismissed, Albert was cut free. He slumped unconscious to the ground, but only momentarily. Cyrus and five other troopers hoisted him up and carried him into the barracks. The regimental surgeon rubbed goose grease into the wounds and remarked that Albert would be as good as new in a short time.

Though the scars would be present forever, no one

in the regiment ever spoke of the incident again, except for one final denouement.

On Albert's third day back in service Lieutenant Dupre called him over. "What was your time from here to Paris?" he inquired.

"Thirteen hours," Albert replied.

The lieutenant whistled softly. "One hundred fifty miles," he observed. "Well, Trooper Penfeld, I think you had better keep Balthasar as your assigned mount."

CHAPTER 7

———— ❧ ————

It was many days before William finally awoke, and when he did the midsummer sun was blazing. When he did awake, he was completely disoriented. "Where am I?" he muttered.

"You are in your own bed, Master William," Samuel answered.

He blinked and squinted slightly swollen eyes, looking quite bewildered. "What happened?" His voice trailed off as his eyes closed. He took a deep breath, clearing a painfully raw throat, and started over. "How did I get here?"

"It is a mystery to all of us," Samuel answered. "Walked? We don't know, but you were mostly dead when I found you." Samuel placed his hand on William's chest. "Don't move. Just rest now. You have lived in a world of nightmares for the past week."

The cook, Maggie, entered the room. "I thought I heard him, poor lad."

"He woke only moments ago."

Maggie picked up a cloth and held it to his mouth. Touching it to his lips, she squeezed out a trickle of water.

William felt its cool refreshment. He licked his lips, swallowed, and opened his eyes again. "Mother?"

The two servants looked at each other woefully. Maggie corrected softly, "No, Master William, it is only me."

"And where is my grandfather?"

"He left for Greenwich early this morning," Samuel reported, "but is due back this evening."

"And my mother? Please send for her," William demanded in boyish petulance.

The pair of servants did not reply. Maggie stared up at the ceiling while Samuel polished an already brilliantly shining coat button. At last Samuel spoke. "She is away."

"Don't be absurd. She was home when I arrived. She never goes out unless accompanied by my grandfather or me. I'm sure she is aware of my condition and must be anxious about me. Why are you keeping her from me? Or what are you keeping from me?" he demanded, his apprehension rising. "Where is she? What's wrong with her?"

When neither of them replied William's mind returned to the devilish morning he had come home. He remembered hearing his mother's voice, but not being able to move. He thought of her ill condition and her weak heart.

Suddenly his memories became clear. The sound of his mother's cry rang in his ears. William sat up. "Mother! Is she ... dead?"

Samuel firmly pushed William back down. "Calm yourself, Master William. Doctor Wilkins has been to see her this morning. He says that she is in no immediate danger, but the shock of seeing you. ... You must realize that your hair and clothing. . ."

Grabbing Samuel's arm, William insisted, "Tell me all, or I shall go find out for myself!"

Samuel looked to Maggie for support, and she nodded. The steward sighed heavily, then said, "Her heart couldn't take the sight. Doctor Wilkins says she is in a coma. She may linger so for some time, and then. . ."

"No!" William screamed, throwing himself violently about the bed. "My blessed, gentle mother."

Maggie tried to soothe him, but her words were drowned out by his agonizing moans. "All of this is on my head! I shall die! I shall surely die!"

He broke down into uncontrollable sobbing, lasting well over an hour. Finally, he slept again.

The next morning William was roused by a booming, angry voice in the hallway. "Is he awake then?"

William groggily heard the argument offered by Maggie outside the bedroom door. "Yes, sir, but he's still very weak and you dare not upset him, or it shall make matters worse."

"You'll not tell me my business in my own house, woman! Leave me at once!"

Silence fell for only a second before William's bedroom door crashed open. And there he was, William's grandfather, banging his heavy boots like hooves on the oak floor and snorting so loudly that William expected to see steam coming from his infuriated breath.

Awkwardly propping himself up in bed on his bandaged hands, William began, "I'm so sor. . ."

"You foul wretch." Sutton's eyes smoldered with the fervent heat of the burning sloop. "You did this to her. You may have killed her!"

"I. . . I. . ." William struggled to get the words out. "But I only came home and was close enough to death myself from trying to save your ship that I. . ."

"Silence! I'll not hear a word from you right now." Lord Sutton towered over the cowering William with a long slender finger pointed right between his eyes. "The very ship *you* burned. I know the truth. No excuse will serve this time. You've cost me a fortune. And more than money. You have taken away the one thing that is sweet and precious to me!"

A tear welled in William's eye and his throat tightened so that he thought he might stop breathing. "But mother's not dead," he croaked.

"My sweet Julia." Lord Sutton's breathing was harsh, and his stance suggested he wanted to strike William right there in bed. "You are a drunk and a gambler. Nothing but a whoring, little thieving beast. You are a disgrace to this family, to yourself, and to God!"

William's feelings hardened now. After all, was he not also devoted to his mother? And what about the burns he had suffered? He decided to let the old man finish, and then he would be done with him and his money, his orders and his condemnations.

"When you're well I want you out, and I never want to see you again." The old man glared into William's eyes. He opened the door and stood holding the knob with as hateful an expression as William had ever seen before. His conclusion was brief before he left the room. "Your middle name is a mockery. That night on the *Hermes*, when you were an infant, I wish to God they'd saved your brother instead. Maybe *his* life would have been worth something."

He slammed the door, leaving William in desolate solitude, his mind empty and numb. He stared blankly, unable even to cry.

William squinted wearily, his eyes taking a long while to adjust to the change of light. The afternoon clientele at Jack Straw's Castle Pub stared at William in a way his money and family connections had never permitted before. The faces were hard and curiously satisfied when they spotted the bulky white bandages wrapping his hands and neck.

One of the men chuckled to others at a corner table. "Seems 'is bloody 'igh-an'-mightiness has finally got what 'e deserves."

William heard the snickers of unanimous agreement. The whole place, even the very walls of Jack Straw's, where only weeks ago he felt he had owned the world, now seemed alien to him.

He walked over to the counter, catching the eye of the barman. "Gin, if you please."

The man eyed him in silence for a moment before pouring the liquor into a dirty glass and slamming it down on the counter.

William drained the glass in a single gulp, then nudged the barkeeper for a refill. "Is Judy here?"

The man looked up from pouring the gin, grunted, and turned away. William leaned over the bar to catch the man's arm. Anxiously he said, "I'm a friend of her's."

"Not anymore!" Beth's abrasive voice corrected from behind him. William turned around. "Did 'e pay yet?" she demanded.

The barman rapped on the counter with his knuckles. "That'll be a shilling, mate."

"A shilling?" William replied with disbelief. "Since when are two gins ever more than sixpence?"

"Since it's ye," Beth said coldly. "Pay and drink up or get out!" she ordered.

"This is no way to treat a valuable customer!" William protested.

Beth barked a sharp, snide laugh. "We 'ave other customers. Anyway, word travels fast 'round 'ere. Yer on the streets."

William could not even convince himself he had the presence that he had once felt. He felt helpless without his money, lower than low. He placed the coin on the counter.

Beth shuffled toward him, poking him in the chest. "And ye can forget about Judy after what ye put 'er through."

"Please," William argued. "If I could just see her."

"She don't wantta see ye! Now drink up and get out."

A man walked through the front door, ducking as he entered. It was Bristol Sims, the man who had confronted William on a previous visit. His knuckles were skinned, and the fading purple remnant of a black eye still marked his face.

"Sims," Beth remarked, "look who's come 'round 'ere lookin' for Judy."

Sims spotted William. "The man who slapped my Judy!" His expression grew instantly angry, then noting William's bandages he began to laugh. "Not so tough now, are we?"

He stepped closer, flicking the bandages on William's hands. Sims was a half foot taller and at least three stone heavier. Even without his injuries, William knew he would have no chance. "I realize," he began to say, but had the air knocked out of him when Sims swung a punch deep into his belly.

William gasped as he fell against the bar, then slid downward. He felt his entire body clench up. He lay on the floor writhing for air and the other men in the bar watched with satisfaction.

"So you like beatin' up on ladies then, do you?!" Sims kicked him in the ribs. William was knocked backward, striking his head against the brass foot rail of the bar.

Sims raised his heavily booted foot to kick him again, but was stopped by Beth. "Look now," she said, holding him back. "You've knocked loose them bandages."

As she spoke William felt the air stinging his raw neck as blood oozed into his shirt collar.

"Stop, or I'll 'ave to clean up 'is bloody mess."

Sims held back in spite of his obvious desire to kick William to death. Instead he grabbed the gin from the counter. "Is this yer drink?!" He yanked William up by his arm, slinging him over the counter. "I said, is this yer drink?"

William nodded quickly, hoping the beating would stop.

"I didn't hear, mate. Maybe ye ought to speak up," Sims said, splashing the drink onto William's burns.

The clear liquid burned cruelly, and William screamed, pulling away.

"All right, enough!" Beth ordered. "Drag 'im out of 'ere. I'll not 'ave the constable botherin' me for allowing this to go on."

Sims grabbed William's coat with both hands, heaved William up over his shoulder, and ran with him. Then as if preparing to throw a javelin, he pitched

William out into the street. William bounced and rolled onto the hard dirt and gravel.

As Sims stood over his crumpled form, William curled his arms and legs, fearful of being kicked again. Bending low beside William's ear, Sims said, "Next time y'send some blokes after Bristol Sims, best make sure an' send enough to do the job. As for ye: come 'round 'ere again, and I'll kill ye."

It was some time before William could drag himself upright and reach his horse. As he stood, holding himself erect by clinging to the stirrup, a flash of red hair and a swinging apron in the doorway caught his eye. It was Judy.

"Judy," he began, but she interrupted.

"I trust you will not annoy me further," she said. "I've got my position and future to think of, and neither of those is things you have now."

CHAPTER 8

"Again!" ordered Lieutenant Dupre. "*Mordioux!* If you execute the wheel in that slipshod a fashion no Englishman will have to shoot me! I will die of embarrassment first! But that will be no comfort to you. I will shoot you myself before dying! Now do it again!"

The rank of troopers, twelve horsemen across, awkwardly reined their fractious mounts to a halt and dressed the line to practice the advance again. When they failed anew, they were treated to a savage lecture by Dupre.

The exercises for new recruits did not let up. For men who had never been on horseback before, the gallant and heroic reputation of the hussars soon included a new reality: it was a lot of hard work. Stable call was at six in the morning, and the mounts were all fed, watered, brushed, and walked before the trooper ever saw a morsel of hard bread. As Dupre was fond of reminding the recruits, new men were expendable, but well-trained horses were valuable and deserved every consideration.

Drill was scheduled every fore- and afternoon. Albert's head felt near to bursting with all the procedures necessary to commit to memory: column by peleton, column serre, battle array. Every formation required a man to know his position, but more important, how to change one into another, often at a gallop. The slightest miscue or hesitation would snarl the entire line and lead to more abuse than Albert ever heard shouted by the fishwives of Paris.

When not drilling on horseback, new recruits practiced with sabers, pistols, and carbines.

Even evenings were not free of instruction. New recruits were not permitted out in the streets of Boulogne until they were considered to be properly indoctrinated in hussar thinking.

"Never allow an insult to pass unremarked—never! No slight to you, your comrades-in-arms, your regiment, or your emperor is permitted!" commanded Henri Bonard to the barracks full of young troopers. Bonard was tall for a hussar, being over six feet in height. He had been a cavalryman since the days of the Revolution and with the regiment for five years. "If you do not immediately receive an apology you must call out the dog upon the instant. Otherwise, never think to return here again!" This was said so ferociously that Bonard's bristling salt-and-pepper moustache quivered with emotion and the saber scar on his cheek turned lividly crimson.

Despite the passionate display, Albert noted that Bonard's braided sidelocks hung down perfectly straight in front of each ear and did not flap at all.

When Bonard left the room and Albert and Cyrus were alone, Cyrus was exultant. "Is this not the finest regiment there is?" he questioned. "What esprit de corps! We are the greatest fighting men in the world!"

"I note you are well on your way to being a credit to the First," Albert commented drily.

"And you are your melancholy self," Cyrus observed. "One would think you would rather be back with the bakers and shop clerks of the Forty-sixth or threading needles in Rue St. Jacques."

When Albert made no response, Cyrus was exasperated. "Weren't you listening?" he demanded. "I've just insulted you. What are you going to do about it?"

"Nothing," Albert replied. "Because I knew you were teasing. Also, you already know I could tear you apart like a fresh baguette. What would be the point?"

Sighing, Cyrus sat on the floor to polish his black

boots. "You do not have the proper spirit," he remarked. "Is it because of Angelique? I hear you murmur her name in your sleep. Yet you never answer her letters, and you told Sergeant Lafere to return them marked 'unknown.' Are you so sick of her that you are trying to forget her? In that case, straighten your plume, *mon ami*, go into town, and let some femme of the Rue du Bras d'Or assist you."

Cyrus was referring to the Street of the Golden Arms; the notorious bordello district of Boulogne.

Albert shook his head. "You could not be more wrong. I love her dearly. I am sick, yes, but sick of not being able to communicate with her. But you alone know the reason. I am not who I thought I was. Worse: I don't even know who I am!"

"But why does it matter so much? You are a dashing trooper of the First Hussars with a bright future. Can't you begin your life now?"

"I have tried to set the past aside, but not knowing torments me! Who were my parents? How did I come to be in the hands of a smuggler? Was he my father, or did he murder my father? What if my parents are still living?"

"Wait, stop a moment," Cyrus suggested with a snap of his fingers. "Did not your grand-mère—pardon,

Madame Heloise—tell you the name of the smuggler and his whereabouts?"

Laughing grimly, Albert agreed. "But what use is that to me? Twenty some years ago, it was."

"Still, it is something to follow up!"

"And how do you suggest I do that? Can I sign out of camp, saying, 'Please excuse me for a fortnight, Colonel, while I ride to Brest to find a smuggler who may not even still be living?" *Ma foi*, it is absurd!"

"But why do you have to go in person? Why don't you get Colonel Rouvillois to write to the Prefecture of Police?"

Albert opened his mouth to offer a scornful reply, then stopped. Pathetic eagerness played over his features. "Do you suppose he would do so?"

"Are the First Hussars a band of brothers? Of course he will! You have but to ask. The gendarmerie of . . . where is it again?"

"Brest."

"The gendarmerie of Brest will be only too pleased—honored—to assist in the researches of a trooper of the celebrated First Hussars."

"But my secret."

"Will remain so! Why should provincial peasants need to know the private affairs of one of his majesty's finest cavalrymen? If your smuggler still exists, a return letter will confirm his whereabouts."

"Cyrus," Albert said with pleased astonishment, "you have achieved perfection. You truly have all the proper attitudes for a trooper of the First Hussars."

Puffed up, Cyrus flicked the sky-blue topknot on the black plume of his shako and adjusted the seams of his trousers.

"There is just one thing you should know," Albert added as he rose to seek the colonel.

"And that is?"

"Did you ever wonder why Bonard is not an officer after a dozen years of service?"

Cyrus's face darkened with suspicion. "And do you know such a thing?"

"*Certainement!* He has been promoted thrice and three times broken back to the ranks for dueling!"

"Certainly you must have some idea," Thomas questioned Lord Sutton. "He is, after all, your grandson. I thought surely you would know where to find him."

"You cannot imagine the circumstances under which we parted," William's grandfather said. Lord Sutton shook his wrinkled brow, mottled red first from anger and then blanched white from the most recent revelation. He paced in his usual spot, near the mantel in the Silver Room. Turning abruptly, he faced the windows as if watching the arrival of someone who was not there. "If what you are saying is true, if William was not the cause of the fire, I'll be as grateful to find him as you."

"And I'm positive I have found the truth. It was bound to leak out at some point."

Lord Sutton looked at Thomas in deep consideration, muttering under his breath, "I'd never have guessed William to be so stupid, but he must be forgiven that, since it nearly caused his own death." He spoke up then. "And how did you hear of this?"

"News of his misfortune reached me when I returned to port from a cruise. I was terrified to think of William's position after such an ordeal, and so I thought I might find his company at Jack Straw's."

Lord Sutton shook his head. "Dreadful place of business."

Thomas nodded in agreement. "Upon arriving at Jack Straw's last night, it was hardly a moment later when several acquaintances hastened to give me details of what really happened."

Lord Sutton's features moved from regret to a more thoughtful look. He leaned both elbows against the mantel, stooping his head. "This dishonorable character. . ."

"Bristol Sims," Thomas interjected.

"Yes, Sims. You say he was in a dispute with William over a woman?"

"And so that all is known, William did cause him to be set upon by ruffians—although it appears he gave as good as he received in that tussle."

"But is that sufficient reason to do murder and arson? Is he such a man that he would do something so barbaric?"

Thomas displayed his concurrence and at the same time quivered with anger. "Oh, yes. I quizzed him myself." He frowned and clenched his teeth. "He is quite a braggart and can keep nothing prideful secret, not even to save his own life. He boasted of following William and the girl to Greenwich, flooding the deck with tar, and setting it ablaze." Thomas shivered.

A look of dread washed over Lord Sutton. He covered his eyes with his hands and groaned, "If only I'd had the patience to listen. Dear God, what have I done? It was not the loss of the ship, you see. It was dear Julia. It drove me mad."

Thomas blurted the words, "I know. To do what you have done..."

Lord Sutton whipped his glance around sharply.

Thomas, realizing his own audacity, stuttered, "I'm

sorry. I understand, or rather can only begin to understand how you must feel."

Lord Sutton softened. "No, Thomas. The anger I feel now is for my own stupidity. Not for you. I deserve far more than words."

"How is the lady Julia?"

"Unchanged, I fear. Hovering in a world of twilight, more dead than alive and yet not dead either . . . waiting . . . ." Lord Sutton shook his head to clear away the vision. "Where can this Sims be found?"

"Jack Straw's, on any day of the week. You may depend upon it."

Brooding, Lord Sutton exclaimed, "Tonight I will send the magistrate and fifty armed men if necessary. What about the girl?"

Thomas gave a dismissive wave. "She is long gone. In fear of Sims, I would surmise, having found that he plotted her death as well as William's. Depend on it: she will survive elsewhere, but is of no consequence to us, or assistance either. But what of William?"

Grandfather Sutton pressed a trembling hand to his chest. "Only God knows. I've sent him, like Uriah the Hittite, alone into the thick of battle to be killed. I would be most grateful for any suggestions you might offer."

Thomas clicked his tongue in frustration. Sims

could easily be taken, but the most important project was finding William. "Have you searched any of your country properties?"

Lord Sutton demurred. "All the buildings are tenant-occupied, or gone derelict. I don't know." He faced Thomas with a look that seemed to place all his hopes on the man. "His mother now hovers just above death. William is all I have left. Help me, Thomas."

Thomas searched the eyes of the broken man.

"Find him for me," Lord Sutton repeated.

Thomas had never seen the proud, stern Lord Sutton so weak, so vulnerable. "I will." He placed his hands on Lord Sutton's spindly arms. "I will," he said again as he urgently rose to take his leave.

Days of interrogating all of William's London acquaintances brought Thomas no closer to discovering the lair of his missing friend. No one had seen him or heard from him—or at least no one would admit it.

Still more days were occupied in searching all of William's known haunts, from his club in St. James to the lowest, seediest dives of the East End. He was nowhere to be found, and even the promise of a lavish expenditure of shillings brought no information. Thomas concluded that if he *were* still alive William was not in London.

Another week of touring Sutton properties brought increasing frustration, and no success. Then, with his shore leave almost expired, Thomas remembered a country cottage to which William had taken him exactly one time very early in their friendship. The building was already a ruin those years earlier and Thomas had little hope that William would have thought it a suitable refuge, but he went there as a last resort.

The Sutton lands and small stone building were located beyond the cathedral town of Ely, Cambridgeshire, some sixty miles from London. Thomas was tired, the rattling coach having taken all night and most of the next day to make the journey. After walking the last two miles across the fens from the high road, Thomas was slightly out of breath as he rapped hard on the plank door. There was no answer. He beat again, harder this time, then leaned his head back into interlaced fingers, looking around while waiting.

The grounds were in a state of disarray. Tall weeds had taken advantage of the summer season to shoot almost up to the low thatch roof. He glanced back at the faint track down which he had come. It too was overgrown with weeds and wildflowers. Any remaining gravel had been washed away with the winter rains, and it looked more like a sheep's trail than any human passage.

"William!" Thomas banged again on the heavy hinged door, trying the latch. "It's Thomas." He waited a moment longer. Sighing unhappily at the vain attempt that had cost him so much effort, he was about to walk away when he heard a noise inside—like a fully loaded tea set had been dropped on stone.

"Go away," a voice croaked.

It was the familiar voice Thomas hoped to hear, though it was clearly not the speech of the William he remembered. "William, open up! I've come a long way, and I did not come to see the weeds in your garden." Shuffling footsteps approached the entry.

"Who is it?" a tongue slurred with drink called out.

"It's Thomas, William. Open up."

Inside the cottage, William staggered toward the door, stumbling over a wicker table. He let out a frustrated yell, picked himself up, kicked the table, and promptly smashed his toe on a fallen brick. "Thomas who?" he yelped.

"Thomas Burton, your best mate!" Thomas said with exasperation. "Now open up before I call a gust of wind to blow down this fortress on your head!"

William unbolted the door. The rusty iron hinges creaked as if they had not been opened in decades. Late afternoon sun beamed directly onto William's face. Beneath the stubble of his whiskers, his skin was as pale as the belly of a lizard, and he cringed painfully in the glare.

"Great thunder, man!" Thomas exclaimed. "You look awful." William's clothes appeared to be tarred to his body. His hair resembled the weeds outside, and his eyes were sunken and filmy. "What happened to you?"

William cracked both eyes to tiny slits to look at his very first visitor. His reaction suggested that ages had passed since he had spoken to anyone. Glaring at Thomas with suspicion, he finally said, "Do you want to come in and have a drink with me, or will you just go away and leave me alone?" Without awaiting a reply, William rubbed his matted hair and turned around.

Narrow beams of light shot across the dark room, illuminating an extraordinary amount of dust and debris. It took a minute for Thomas's vision to adjust. The cottage reeked of liquor and other odors too foul to describe. He searched for a place to rest his weary bones. William plunked down on a grimy mattress that sprawled in the corner on the floor.

"So this is the way you keep yourself when I go away," Thomas said cautiously.

William laughed. "Dear Thomas, I've been a terrible

wreck since you left. That lousy tart Judy," he began, but Thomas motioned for silence.

"I know, I know. I heard everything." He looked at William with sorrowful eyes.

"Ah," William grunted. "The fire and all." Then, "How did you find me?"

"I came into London on leave, and when I heard about what happened, I paid a visit to your grandfather."

"Oh really, and how is the old sod?"

"Really quite worried about you."

"Worried! He's the one to blame for all this." William searched for the words. Frustrated and angry he said, "I never liked him anyway. I've gained my independence now, and I don't need him." He flung himself back on the mat and looked around the dingy room with satisfaction.

Thomas bobbed his head and permitted a chuckle to escape his lips. "Indeed."

William stared down at himself, lifting a limp, stained shirttail. "I'm in a rough state, but when I get this place cleaned up. . ."

"I think you should torch it," Thomas interjected.

William's face took on a serious look. "You think so? Burn it to the ground, shall I? Once an arsonist, always so? I would, you see, but the stones wouldn't burn."

Thomas gently kicked an empty wine bottle with

his foot. "If you threw enough of these corks on the flames they would."

William's grin slipped away at the remembrance of his lengthy drunken state. Suddenly he was embarrassed for Thomas to see him that way. "It's been a long summer," he said, hoping Thomas would understand.

"I know." Thomas patted his shoulder. "Listen, there's something I've got to tell you. It's the reason I came all the way out to see you."

"What? Not just for my sparkling company?" William replied sarcastically.

"None of what happened can be blamed on you."

"You came all this way to tell me that? I knew it beforehand; I've been reminding myself of that since I left. Try telling it to my grandfather."

"I have already."

That comment brought an attentive look to William's face.

"I mean it," Thomas continued. "You know that slime named Sims, at Jack Straw's?"

William's brow wrinkled. "Mmm? The one I paid three gents to beat the daylights out of? The one who paid me back in the same coin?"

Thomas grinned. "The very same."

"Why?"

"You did wrong to set the dogs on him, but now I

think you may consider that as a prepayment for later sins."

William was puzzled. "What?"

"Listen. Sims was bragging about the fire on the *Stronghold*. I interviewed him myself, posing as your enemy, and while pretending to get pickled with him, he confirmed it to me in the most direct way."

"He did?" William jumped from his seat, tripping over his own legs. "Are you sure? What did he say?"

"He bragged about 'having his own back again.' Said he'd not only cost you pain but even gotten you 'turned out,' as he so elegantly phrased it."

William was lost for words.

Thomas grew more serious and bit his lip. "I had great difficulty not smashing his face right there, but I thought I would go to your grandfather first."

William's face darkened as he relived the horrific event of the ship burning.

"He's probably been arrested by now and will rot or hang, with the power Lord Sutton has."

William let out a sigh as if even hearing his grandfather's name tortured him.

"He was so apologetic when he found he'd wronged you," Thomas argued persuasively. "He wished he'd never done what he did. I've never seen him so weak. I thought he would cry. He even said that you were all he had left."

"He was powerfully quick to believe ill of me! He is nothing to me! He doesn't even exist. As far as I'm concerned, my mother. . ." William stopped abruptly as the full impact of Thomas's words struck him. "You mean my mother is dead then? And I missed her funeral."

Thomas corrected him by saying encouragingly, "No, William, she's not dead, but still deeply in a coma."

William shrugged. Looking into his friend's pale-blue eyes he said, "As good as dead then."

Thomas knew it was a sore subject, so he let it rest. "Your grandfather wants you back. He told me he had humbled himself, approached Lord Cornwallis again, and got him to agree to offer you a commission if I could find you."

"Swear to me, Thomas, that you'll not tell him where I am," William demanded fiercely. "I am not ready to see him again. I may never be. Swear it!" He knew Thomas had no choice. They had grown up together, on many occasions risking much for each other. Thomas's first loyalty would always be to William, near brother and closest friend for life.

Thomas paused long in consideration. "I promised him. May I at least tell him that you live?"

William drew his head back slowly, as if suspecting his friend's allegiance.

"But I won't if you insist, William."

"Good." William was relieved. "I don't care about his bloody commission anyway. I never want another thing from that old ram. To sail would mean to be like him, and that is the last thing I want. Uh, and how is the king's navy treating you then?"

"It's fine. I had a quiet first tour, but we still took two prizes. I have a few coins in my pocket." He peered through the doorway at the setting sun. "And one day to be back aboard ship. I must be off again."

"But you've only just arrived," William protested.

"I know, but I must be back in London by tomorrow night. We're making sail at nine o'clock."

"Won't you at least have a drink with me before you go?" William looked around for a bottle that was not empty.

"Thank you, no. You should consider carrying less of a load yourself."

William shrugged.

"But, before I go, I wonder if you remember the village not too far from here. Branson Fen, I believe it's called."

"I remember," William allowed. "The inn there

furnishes all my needs." He nudged a clay cider jug with his toe.

"Besides that," Thomas corrected. "That quiet little church there. I'll bet there are some good people who can help."

"No, you don't," William said flatly. "If you think I'll go back after all God has put me through. . ."

Thomas held up his hands to disengage from argument. It was just a suggestion, if you should ever need someone." He stood as he concluded, "I don't think God is to be blamed for your condition as much as thanked that you are still alive."

William smiled at his friend's concern. Thomas had always been there for him. Thomas approached to shake his hand, but William ignored it, giving him a stout hug instead. "Thank you for being my friend, Thomas."

They parted. William felt a lump in his throat. Thomas already had to leave after too short a time. "Take care of yourself," he called. "Mind that the French do not part your hair with a musketball."

Thomas nodded and called out, "Think about that church."

William watched his friend's dwindling form as the sun sank, taking with it his heart. Night fell, and with it arrived deep loneliness.

CHAPTER 9

———— ❧ ————

Albert squatted next to the tiny campfire, prodding it with a thin stick and studying the center of the glowing embers. The light danced on his face, distorting it strangely, casting a shadow upward from his chin, darkening his eyes. Cyrus lay opposite the blaze, resting against his pack, reading a letter.

The sea air was brisk for August, Albert thought idly, trying to forget the day's battle. The First Hussars had fought and won a bloody skirmish hours before. The loss of soldiers was severe, but Colonel Rouvillois assured them it was victory. Now they made their encampment on the very field they had fought for.

Most soldiers were already sleeping, exhausted from the long march and fighting behind them, and the prospect of more of the same to come. Albert mused over his useless discovery: the *thought* of going on makes you tired. "What else would it do?" he mumbled, rocking back on his heels and settling to the ground with a *thump*.

"Mmm?" Cyrus gazed up from his letter.

"I said, we should rest. We've a long march ahead." Albert turned to his pack behind him and untied the bedroll.

"Albert," Cyrus said, "this letter that I always read, don't you ever wonder about it?"

"It's your business. I wouldn't want to bother you."

"I will tell you what it is, since you won't ask. My mother sent it."

"Oh? Why has she not sent more?"

Cyrus ran his hand through dirty hair as his eyes fell to the ground. "I do not know, but I can imagine. Albert, our families have difficulties as well. The war may even be harder for them than for us."

"Listen," Albert cautioned, "I know what you are trying to say, but it's none of your business."

"But why would you neglect Angelique? It isn't her fault."

Albert's temper was rising. "I say once more, Cyrus, my business is mine and none of yours."

"I have the letters she sent. I think you should read..."

Albert rose abruptly and glared at Cyrus with his fists clenched. "What?"

"I said I have been saving the letters, and I think the matter is of great importance to you."

A moment of silence followed except for a light breeze that hissed through the treetops as if trying to shush Cyrus. Albert strode to where Cyrus lay, gathered up his shirtfront, and heaved him to his feet. "You didn't send the letters back? You've *read* the letters?"

"A-Albert," Cyrus stuttered, "I know ..." His excuse was cut short by a sharp blow that landed squarely on his mouth, cutting his lips on both upper and lower teeth.

Albert backed Cyrus around the campfire, pursuing him with fists held high. Cyrus retreated, holding one hand to his battered mouth, gesturing for Albert to stop with the other. "She writes so insistently," Cyrus said, "I knew it must be important."

"It is not yours to know!" Albert rushed him, falling on top of him. Albert threw blow after blow at his face.

Cyrus shielded himself with his arms wrapped over his head. Twisting and wriggling under Albert, he cried out, "She's pregnant!"

The barrage of punches halted. Albert remained over Cyrus, arms poised for attack, as a look of bewilderment slid down his face. His jaw dropped open. "What?"

Cyrus opened his defense and repeated the words softly, "She is pregnant."

Albert looked away into the darkness beyond the encampment and slumped over, off of Cyrus. "How long?" he asked, still panting from the brawl.

"At least three weeks she has known. I am truly sorry I read them, I only. . ."

Albert responded, "No, I'm glad you did. I'm sorry that. . ."

Cyrus held up his hands to stop him. "I understand, I'd have done the same."

They sat together without speaking for a while, Albert contemplating his family, Cyrus smiling and lightly poking at his swollen, bloodied lips, congratulating himself on finally getting through to Albert.

Then Cyrus said, "I don't understand one thing. Why were you refusing the letters?"

Albert rubbed his eyes. "You know why. I found out I am not who I thought I was. I was ashamed. I'm a fraud. My beliefs, my accomplishments, my entire life. Every one looks at me and loves me as something I'm not. I'm not brave, I'm not. . ."

Cyrus interrupted, "Albert, no one thinks you are perfect. These men, your family, your friends—we all love you because you are *real*. We know you have doubts and fears, but the way you charge through them is what we love about you. You are an example to live up to because you have the same problems as anyone else, but you master them."

Albert smiled and looked over at his friend. "And now?" he asked. "How do I master this? A few weeks ago, I might have returned home, but not now. The army would never let me go. We're moving too much, fighting too often."

"I'll dispatch a letter to Paris tomorrow, delivering your apology and fifty francs. That should help her until you return."

"Ah, Cyrus." Albert clasped his shoulder, and the impact made Cyrus flinch, briefly recalling the earlier fight. Albert laughed. "You think of everything. But let me write the letter. I owe her the truth."

But on the morrow, the First Hussars found itself the advance guard on the long road to the Rhine. There was no chance to even send a letter.

William's head was pounding. He walked gingerly down the dirt road toward Branson Fen as if fearful his legs would betray his weight. His bones ached, and he was stiff. It was the first morning in weeks he had not been three parts drunk before noon since coming to Cambridgeshire. It was not a matter of a new resolve however; he was staggering toward the village to replenish his supply of liquid cure-all: more alcohol. His thoughts were slow and deliberate, and he felt so lonely that he began to talk aloud.

"What can one say when one has no one to say anything to?"

He answered himself. "One could first say hello."

"Very well then. Hello." He thought about the emptiness that came with saying hello to one's self for lack of having someone else there. If a conversation with one's self, he thought, was going to be the least bit inviting, the two voices should at least have names of their own so as to keep track of who was who.

"Agreed," one voice said. "I shall be Charles."

"And I shall be William."

It interested him vaguely that the first name chosen was that of his long-dead and half-forgotten twin brother. But having no associations to make with the name of the vanished sibling, he ruminated over another Charles and decided on King Charles the Second; the king known for his passionate love of parties and women.

"It is me to the very core," he muttered. "But what of you, William?" he asked himself. "What sort of character traits fit you? What is a William expected to be like?"

"Strong and courageous," one voice answered. "Like William the Conqueror."

"Bah!" he retorted. "That William is unlike anything I've seen of myself in a long while. He has gone away into hiding and has remained there since I was a child. All that is truly left of that William is the name, and even that is a facade for covering up the Charles in you. The life of Charles will always be my first choice," William spoke aloud.

The new game was one that William found he enjoyed, as if pleased to find his brain still functioning after its long stupor. He thought of other people whose names could be linked to their character, and this led him to Thomas and what a gentle soul and true friend he was, and how firmly he held to his beliefs. This notion reminded him of St. Thomas à Becket. "What a man he must have been to die for what he believed, virtually by the hand of the king, his supposed friend." William thought of the dedication to God Archbishop Becket must have had. "What immovable faith," he said aloud. "To hold fast to the principles of the church even against the will of the king." William refused to credit the idea. "You would never catch me taking a stand like that," he told himself.

The voice of Charles agreed. "For a man to have everything in the world and then to lose his life over something like principles! Pure foolishness!"

This thought struck him as more odd than the first.

William realized that the happiness this man had was not from his worldly position or possessions, but from being given over wholly to the will of God.

William considered this, but quickly chased away the notion that God could make him happy.

"God is for the weak-minded who need something to lean on," he heard the voice of Charles say.

Instead he reminded himself of the things that had made him happy before the recent troubles: gambling, drinking, carousing. How could devotion to God possibly be a substitute for the joys of the flesh?

Reviewing the good times, his mind took him from his first drink, his first kiss, and his first turn at hazard, through the course of the events that followed, all the way up to the present. The voice he had come to recognize as William pointed out, "And the pain you have now is because of all those things."

He argued the point. "No. It can't be." It was only circumstances that led to the ruin, William insisted, but the other argument crept in again.

"If you weren't gambling, you wouldn't have met Judy. If you hadn't been consumed with lust for her, you wouldn't have been set up by Sims, and on and on. And if it weren't for the drink, you wouldn't still be here, stinking as you are, and planning to remain so. Instead you would be somewhere making a name for yourself like Thomas à Becket and like the way your friend Thomas is right now. You would be doing something with your life, instead of wasting it."

Then the voice of Charles crushed him with despair. "But it's too late. Your chances of being an officer at sea are far gone. Your father and brother have been dead for all your life. Your mother is near death now, if not dead already. And what of your grandfather, the source of your wealth? He has thrown you out and taken away all that was good. There is nothing left for you to live for. No money, no women, no ships at sea, no future—nothing left except a slow death on the bottle."

William grew depressed as he walked along the road. The branches of the trees were restless, like the voice inside his head that said, "Why don't you take care of it? There is no point in going on this way."

He passed a rocky cliff along which the road ran. Examining its height, William allowed hopelessness to sweep over him. The voice of Charles insisted, "Look there! You can do it now! Throw yourself off the cliff. It won't even hurt but a moment, and you shall be out of all your pain and uselessness."

William moved closer to the edge, asking himself what he had to live for. He called out to God, "I want to have a purpose in life! Show me, Lord."

The wind rustled again in the trees as a heavy cloud

darkened the sky. "Prove to me, Lord, that I should endure another day."

Expecting to see lightning strike a tree, he waited as he moved closer to the abyss. Waited to hear an immensely loud voice tell him not to jump, to offer him a future that held a better life. He held himself in expectation as some minutes passed. When no such announcement came, he decided he would jump after all.

At the last instant he cried, "Show me now, Lord, or I shall surely kill myself!"

Wind blasted up from the ravine and into his face. It seemed to hold him back. His body swayed from its force. He was paralyzed, and a whisper came to him. This time it was not the voice of Charles, William, or his own. It was much more powerful and spoke with authority. *I hear your cries, William. I see the pains of your past and present, and only I know where you will be tomorrow.*

A vibrating warmth surrounded his body. William felt dizzy with fear, and he closed his eyes.

You must trust in me. It is in my plan that you will do great things, but first you must look for me in the small ways I present myself to you. Only then will you know what I have for you to do.

The voice faded away with the wind, and William was left trembling. When he opened his eyes, he was amazed to find that somehow he had been moved, carried from the edge of the cliff to the embankment of the road. He was alive and safe, his back pressed against solid rock, though he could not recall walking. He stood awestruck. His head and the whole world seemed to be clear, but his attention was drawn to the sound of a carriage approaching from around the bend.

Just as he spied the open-topped conveyance, pulling into the long straightaway, he heard a crack. The right front wheel bounced hard over a rock before it sagged and bowed. Flattening, splinters shot in all directions.

The carriage tipped forward as if it would roll, bouncing twice and grinding the axle stub into the clay road. The driver clung to the seat. He was almost rattled loose as the naked hub plowed a long streak.

The coach skidded to a stop inches from the side of the cliff that William had almost leaped from. He watched in horror as the carriage teetered on the verge of the precipice.

The driver whipped at the horses. They strained, leaning into the harness and neighing fearfully, but the carriage was hung up on the lip of the ravine. Sensing it could topple at any moment, William sprinted across the road and latched onto the uptilted side of the carriage. The horses' eyes rolled wildly, and their hooves churned frantically.

"Help me!" the driver called.

"Jump clear!"

The older man dressed in black clambered for the high side of the seat.

"Hurry!" William shouted. "It's sliding!"

The man leaped from the driver's box as the carriage slipped a bit more. He landed hard on the ground and rolled heavily. "Hold on, son, while I cut the horses loose!"

With William struggling to keep from being dragged with the rig into the canyon, the man scurried beneath the traces, pulled a clasp knife from his pocket, and began to cut.

"It's too heavy!" William called. "It's going to take me with it!" His boots lost their hold, and he was dragged toward the rim.

Finally a trace ripped loose, flying violently backward and slapping the side of the carriage. With this the carriage's weight shifted, and it began to roll. The splintered forewheel caught William in the belly and snagged him fast. William felt himself going over the brink.

Then the driver cut the remaining line, and the horses went staggering forward, stumbling.

As the carriage turned, the man dove for William's feet, grabbing them tightly, as William was almost flung into the air. The axle stub ripped free of his clothing. The two fell to the ground as the carriage tumbled fatally into the ravine. It bounced from rock to rock, shattering to fragments, before the pieces came to rest some hundred feet below.

Breathless, William looked at the man. He was a healthy sixty, and he had short gray hair, pale skin, and pale-blue eyes. He had a look that William could only describe as a reverent calmness.

The man stared back gratefully. "Thank you," he said, panting. "I don't know what would have happened had you not come along."

William smiled, remembering the voice only moments before. "I'm glad I was here too." He looked at the horses.

The older man pointed at them. In a kind, thick Welsh accent he said, "I'm certain I would have lost them. That would have been dreadful."

William agreed. "A good matched pair is hard to find."

"Yes," the man agreed. "They're also the only pair that the congregation has."

"Congregation?" William inquired.

"Yes, the Church of St. Thomas at Branson Fen. The church has only lately purchased them for the use of the militia. We are preparing for the French invasion, of course."

"Invasion? For certain this time?"

The man nodded. "You've not heard then? Have you been livin' in a cave these past months or somethin'?"

"Of sorts," William said. "But when is it coming?"

"Soon perhaps. Napoleon has gathered more than three hundred thousand troops and is ready to attack as soon as his fleet can break the blockade. God save England from that, but if he does, I'll not have my grandchildren speakin' French." The man's spirit lit up. "Two dozen men we've got, with pitchforks and pickaxes. They'll fight to defend His Majesty's fen country."

The news was a shock to William. He'd never imagined the danger would come so close to home. He looked blankly out over the ravine, wondering why Thomas had said nothing of this.

The man stretched out his hand. "I'm Father Donspy." The priest invited William to supper after services the following day. William sensed something about the man he really liked, a kind of instant admiration and respect, a feeling of comfort.

Without pretension, Father Donspy thanked God for saving his and the horses' lives.

Although he did not remark on it at the time, William also recognized it as an answer to his prayers. Before parting he asked, "And which St. Thomas is your parish honoring, Father? The apostle?"

"No," Donspy corrected. "It calls to mind the deeds of the holy martyr, St. Thomas of Canterbury. Becket was his surname. Anglo-Saxon he was, and raised hereabouts."

William and Father Donspy walked toward Branson Fen, each leading one of the horses. The sun was warm, the day becoming pleasant. William was loath to speak about himself in the light of the guilt he carried, but Father Donspy had a way of gently draining the truth from someone, rather than pumping it. He was kind and so easy to talk to that soon William discovered he was recounting how he'd become a gambler, a liar, and had a love for the drink. The priest expressed no revulsion or disgust and showed such compassion that William could not help responding. It was natural then to carry the tale up to what had happened just an instant before they met.

"Do you think God spoke to me, Father?"

"I am certain of it," Donspy responded, "and I am glad he took his time about it. You see, what if you and he had finished your conversation before I came along? You would not have been there for my crisis."

This was a strange thought for William: that he, wretch that he was, had been dispatched to serve God? And that God's seeming lack of attention had really been an instance of immaculate timing? The notion made William's head swim.

To cover the awkwardness, William inquired about Donspy's views on the war. To his surprise, he discovered the priest was quite an activist and planned to fight with the volunteers should the invasion come.

"And do you expect to be attacked here, so far in the country?"

"Stands to reason, doesn't it?" Donspy said with gusto. "Why would Boney attack where he is expected? Landin' by ship can be anywhere, eh? What better than in the Wash, here in the east country, then a sweep southward to catch our defenses from behind."

"I have seen Napoleon's troops in Italy," William said. "They are tough and well disciplined. Surely it would be better to negotiate with Napoleon. What do we care about what happens to the continent if he will leave us alone here?"

Donspy stopped and laid his hand on William's arm. His brows were bristling with suppressed emotion. "Young man," he said. "Foolishness is a part of youth, but some things are best not even spoken of lightly. Would you negotiate with the devil? And if you satisfied his demands this year, what would you give up when he came again the next? Would anyone have done pilgrimage to honor the sainted Becket if he had 'negotiated' with tyranny back in his day? Evil must be met head-on. It does not ever lessen with time but only grows."

William was glad then that he had not spoken disparagingly of the military, along with everything else he had admitted.

The square tower of the Church of St. Thomas à Becket came into view over the elms. Donspy left off lecturing and gestured toward it with pride. "The choir is Anglo-Saxon stonework," he said. "Built, oh, in the year 1000, say. The rest is Norman and mentioned in the Domesday Book."

There was a crowd milling around the churchyard, worried about the missing vicar. "We thought you was mebbe captured by the French," said a scarecrow-shaped man identified as Lem the sexton. "Or did you catch you a French spy?"

Donspy chided Lem and the others for having overactive imaginations and shooed them inside the building for the noon Mass. It was clear that no one was going to be paying attention to the worship until William's presence was explained, so Donspy told of the accident on the cliff, calling William "one sent by God in time of need."

William was blushing with embarrassment at his ragged, unkempt appearance. He was so busy trying to act agreeable that he was still nodding when Donspy said something about how William had studied the movements of the French army and as a born-gentleman was obviously just what the Branson Fen militia needed to prepare to repel the invasion.

His head snapping around in mid-nod, William opened his mouth to protest when he realized that Donspy had in that instant transitioned into the service proper. There was no graceful way to interrupt, but William made up his mind that as soon as the meeting ended he would clear up any misunderstanding about his role in any military playacting.

With the words of the benediction still ringing in his ears, William tried to push through the crowd to speak to the preacher. His progress was slowed by all those who stopped to thank him for saving their priest's life and for volunteering to train the militia.

When William finally reached the parson, Donspy was facing the other way and speaking to a pair of women. Impatient to get the confusion resolved, William broke in on the conversation. "Pardon me, Father," he said, "but there is something I want to clear up immediately. You see, I . . ."

"Ah, William," Donspy said, pivoting abruptly and drawing the young man by the hand. "I want you to meet my wife and daughter. Emily, Dora, this is the man whom God specially appointed for today."

William tried to continue to protest, but the words would not come. The Donspy womenfolk were both petite and smiling, with perfectly clear skin. And eighteen-year-old Dora's soft blonde ringlets framed the most beautiful, heart-shaped face William had ever seen. Wide-open dark eyes regarded William with interest and gratitude.

"We were just discussin' the militia trainin' scheduled for this afternoon," Donspy said smoothly. "There is plenty of time for us to eat first, of course, and Emily was sayin' that perhaps you would like to bathe. How stupid of me not to notice. Your tussle with the coach and horses has played merry ned with your clothin', but I think some of mine could be pressed into service until yours can be cleaned. Is that agreeable? Come along, come along, let us show you to the vicarage."

Bathed, shaved, and clothed, William was treated to a sumptuous meal in which all the Donspys proved as adept at drawing out information as the good father. William found himself speaking with comfortable familiarity of sailing terms, of outlandish foreigners and exotic animals. Miss Donspy seemed to hang on his every word, and her sensible questions showed the intelligence behind the matchless face. To his own surprise, William discovered he wanted very much to impress her.

When the meal had come to all too sudden a conclusion, William was escorted to the village green. While
the ladies retreated outside the stone fence, William was
approached by an odd-looking fellow with big lips.
Duncan Harvey, a man with deep wrinkles and a big red
nose, was the self-styled commander of the Branson Fen
Militia. "Good day to you, Cap'n," he said in a heavy
east-country accent, sounding as if his gums were sewn
to his cheeks and his tongue too thick for his mouth.

William shook his hand. "I'm William Sutton. It's a
pleasure to meet you."

"Pleasure's all mine, Cap'n. We've waited a long time
for you to come. I asked Father Donspy months ago
could he locate a real military man to help with the
trainin'. What with the invasion only around the bend,
as it were, I'd say hit's about time you showed up."

William chuckled, thinking Duncan must be teasing
him. How on earth could he have been expected? And
a real military man at that? William looked around at the
three dozen men standing with turf spades and wooden
pitchforks and almost began to laugh. When he saw that
Duncan was serious, he quickly straightened up, particularly since Miss Donspy and her mother were watching expectantly from the shade. "Yes, well, sorry."

"I'm glad you've finally got your priorities straight,

Cap'n. This town needs you. Right. Shall we review the troops?"

What else could William say except, "By all means."

Duncan began with as much enthusiasm as a country squire discussing his pack of hunting dogs. "We've got thirty-five men, countin' me. And over here is our secret weapon." He walked William to a canvas-draped object previously unseen behind the crowd. Breaking out of their uneven ranks at once, the other thirty-four men crowded around their heels like puppies.

When Duncan tossed aside the tarpaulin with a flourish, William had to struggle to keep from chortling.

"Here she is," Duncan boasted, patting the barrel of a small brass cannon, only three feet high and green with verdigris. "Left behind on Scarlet Island when the navy landed at Zeeland and took Denmark's fleet away at Copenhagen. Hit was a glorious victory for us on that day."

William remembered well hearing his grandfather talk of the battle, though, according to Lord Sutton, it was anything but glorious. It was in fact one of the worst international political moves Britain could have made. The nation lost respect over the matter in Europe, and as Grandfather Sutton had quoted Lord Grey, the ships taken "was of poor compensation for such an act of violence and injustice."

"Anyroad," Duncan continued, "this piece was donated like by a lieutenant who saw action in that affair. From this very parish, he was. Had it crated and shipped here to be a memorial to his family. Only Father Donspy says, 'Don't spike that gun. We may have need of hit someday'—and there you are. And may I be hung for lyin' if that hain't the straight of hit."

William laughed. "Bravo, then. Hurrah for Father Donspy."

Duncan concurred, approaching the men and nodding with vitality. They, in turn agreed unanimously, bobbing their heads as if all were attached to the same puppet string.

William examined the brass-barreled gun. The object in question, a four-pound gun, could jokingly be styled "field artillery," but William thought it might be easier to sling it over one's shoulder than drag it behind a horse. This too he did not say. "All right then, let us see what you can do with it."

With this suggestion, Duncan eyed him cautiously. "Well, Cap'n," he whispered, taking William by the arm and walking him away from the group, "we've never actually fired the thing. You see the only munitions we have is for muskets of which we have none. But, not wantin' to discourage the men, I told 'em how it was too soon, and they must learn their drill first." No more than two inches separated Duncan's bulbous nose from William's sharply pointed one. "You'll not be tellin' 'em differnt, now?"

William shook his head seriously, noticing that the militiamen were leaning forward in their strain to over-hear the conversation. When they saw William watching them, they all pivoted in different directions, the picture of total innocence.

William edged closer to Duncan and whispered back, "This is much like the swivel guns on my family's ships. I've got a plan."

Duncan flipped his head sideways and pushed his ear right against William's mouth. "Give it here, Cap'n," he pleaded.

"Have one of your men retrieve the powder."

Duncan instantly spun around and shouted, "Private Megahey! Retrieve the powder keg!"

Megahey sprinted toward a storage shed at a full gallop, and Duncan pressed his ear to William's mouth once more.

William continued, "Have him get a sack of musketballs too."

"Private Megahey! Halt!"

Megahey skidded to a stop, almost sliding off his own feet.

"Get shot too!"

Megahey took off at a run again.

"And have him bring flint and steel too."

At one hundred times the volume, Duncan relayed the orders. "Megahey!"

The youth halted just feet from the shed and started back.

"Don't forget flint and steel too!"

Megahey was so eager and bolted so quickly that he ran straight into a wooden beam jutting over the door of the shed. He collapsed, senseless.

Shouting at the top of his lungs, Duncan guided the men through their first crisis. "Wounded man on the field!" At this command, fourteen others took off for Megahey. Each of them grabbed a portion of a limb, threatening to dismember him as they carted him off into the shade.

William was amused. "Right," he exclaimed with his finger in the air. "We've got a whole column of Frenchmen attacking and only one gun. Now what are we going to do?" He proceeded to answer his own question. "This weapon is much like the defensive cannon carried aboard merchant ships, and I have some knowledge of their use." He eyeballed the sack of gunpowder and ordered a charge rammed down the throat of the gun.

Next he indicated the sack of musketballs. "Now

ram this down the barrel." William poured a trickle of powder into the touchhole.

One of the men spoke up. "But where are the French?"

It was a valid point. Now that he had the gun loaded, what could he shoot? William spied a tumble-down barn facing them across a nearby field. "Whose is that?" he asked, pointing.

Duncan stepped up and answered knowledgeably, "Hit's old Patrick Swan's."

"What's in it?"

"Swan!" shouted Duncan. "What's in the barn?"

An old man, looking to be in his seventies and still not the oldest of the group, stepped forward and answered in a strained, moaning voice, "Naught. It's empty cause I'm plannin' ta build me new."

William's eyes lit up. "Commander Harvey! The French are in that barn. Permission to shoot."

Duncan saluted him stiffly, then called to Swan. "Swan! The French are in your barn!"

"What?!!!" Swan replied with a twitch of his eyebrows. "The French are in my barn? Blast it. Blast it!"

William ordered the gun wheeled into position and elevated the barrel with a wedge of wood. "Stand to the side."

All the men backed away. Several of them had to

restrain Swan from running out onto the field as he shouted, "Fire, fire at the French! Don't let 'um take my barn!"

"It's all yours," William said, handing flint and steel to Duncan.

Commander Harvey pondered the alignment, then scraped the flint against the steel just above the bowl of powder on top of the magazine. It sizzled, and an instant later, as Harvey jumped clear, it exploded with all the enthusiasm of a first-rate, seventy-four-gun double broadside.

Smoke filled the air. A second later the charge struck the corner of the old, rickety wooden barn precisely where William had aimed. Chunks of wood splintered in all directions. The crack of the building echoed back with the rolling thunder of the cannonfire returning. The building tipped a bit toward them and stopped.

Everyone was frozen, fixed in place. The structure tipped more and began to creak. No one moved, except for old Swan who shouted, "You got the French right in the side!"

The barn leaned a bit more. And then it happened all at once. Now missing a corner, the "French" barn came crashing to the ground, sending a cloud of dust rolling out, causing everyone to cheer.

"Grapeshot," William explained. "Very effective against massed enemy formations."

All the men piled around William to congratulate him on his victory. Some wanted to make him the new commander, but William tactfully declined. "I will be pleased to be of whatever assistance I can," he said.

The smile on Dora Donspy's face was enough reward for one day.

Chanting as if William were Joshua and Jericho had just been leveled, the militia finally set him down under the shade of a huge elm. Glowing all over, the positive attention made him feel as if he were the schoolboy hero of a cricket match. He forgot what was behind him. A line of a dozen or so admirers formed in front of him, all talking at once.

The pleasant camaraderie was interrupted by a big, heavyset fellow with a shock of white hair and a scowl on his face.

"What's a young dandy like yourself come here for anyway?" the man quizzed. "I don't take kindly to strangers, myself, without there be a few questions answered, and neither should the rest of you, if you ask me."

A giant of a woman, towering over the assembly, interrupted. "Oh, Roland. There now! He saved Vicar Donspy from a nasty fall. That's good enough for me. It's none of your business where he comes from."

"And what of this is your business, Daisy Whitby?" the white-haired interrogator threatened.

It came to William that if Daisy Whitby had lived in an earlier age she might have been named *Mighty She-Oak* and been called on to repel the incursions of the Vikings. She would make a crack deterrent against the French invasion. One look at her face and the troops of Napoleon would turn back to fairer damsels.

William protested, "Really, Miss Whitby, it is understandable he should want to know more."

"Oh no, 'tisn't," she insisted, grasping William's arm and leaning uncomfortably close. "You're just jealous, Roland, because dear Mister Sutton here has all the attention you once had."

Roland growled, neither denying nor confirming the accusation. "Fickle female! Out of my face, woman." And he stomped off, leaving the crowd to mutter that this was certainly the end of Roland's affection for Daisy. William had won her great and passionate heart.

"I was right. He was jealous of you, Mister Sutton," she gloated. "I am Miss Daisy Whitby, and I am pleased to make your acquaintance. They say you are from Hampstead. Do you have a lady friend back in Hampstead? Come here now, tell me about yourself." She clamped his hand into her own just as William spotted Dora Donspy.

"A pleasure to make your acquaintance, Miss Whitby. Another time, perhaps. Ah, yes, I see someone with whom I must have a word," he said, kissing Miss Whitby on her hand, then darting over to the young woman.

He took Dora by the arm. "Good afternoon, Miss Donspy. It's good to see you." He walked her quickly away, glancing back to see if the woman was following. Daisy only batted her lashes coyly as William made his escape.

Gorgeous young Dora was confused by the situation. "What's wrong?" she asked, sensing William's urgency.

"That woman behind me. She is rather forward."

Dora looked right into William's apprehensive eyes and laughed. "Oh, dear. Daisy," she said, chuckling. "I hate to disappoint you, but she does that with every man she sees."

"Believe me," William assured her, "it's no disappointment, as long as you keep me away from her!"

Dora laughed at the funny face he made, and her laughter tinkled like the sound of harness bells. William caught himself staring at her. She was one of the most beautiful creatures on earth, yet unpretentious and not in the least artificial. She was not like the ones with too-tight dresses, drenched in rosewater so thick it would make bees swarm in winter. Dora's beauty was more fragile and yet somehow more enduring.

William caught a glance from Father Donspy. It was not a harsh or forbidding glance, not overly protective, but considerate and thoughtful. It was William's own conscience, knowing what Donspy knew about him, that made him flush to be seen talking to the vicar's daughter. He stumbled over his next few words about life in Branson Fen, but Dora smoothly took up the flow.

"Oh, I love it here," Dora said. She looked around at the green hills and the stone cottages. "I was born here and have never left. I've not been anywhere else. I suppose it must seem terribly mundane and common to one as traveled as you."

"Not at all, Miss Donspy, I assure you," William said with all the fervor he could muster. "I have found great warmth and beauty right here." Totally engulfed in her words and her eyes, William dreamed of taking this young princess out of the tiny little town and showing her the world, giving her everything, when reality struck him. He had no home, no money, no world to show. He vowed that he would someday, but for now all he could offer her was humble honesty.

"Tell me more about London," Dora requested. "Is it grand?"

"It is," William agreed. "But truly some of the most

wonderful parts are the parks and green spaces. Take Greenwich on the river. There's a hill near the Royal Naval College all green with tall grass and wildflowers. In the afternoons couples climb to the top for picnics. There are also lots of old sailors with telescopes set up, and for a few pence they'll show you just about anything in the city. St. Paul's cathedral, even the hill of Hampstead where I used to live." Hurrying on he added, "It's a lot of work getting to the top, good exercise you know, but the part I like is coming back down. When I've looked my fill and rested a bit, I like to run down as fast as I can. At the bottom I'm usually moving so fast, I end up tumbling in the grass and flowers." William's face glowed with good cheer even as he wondered to himself why he had not thought about such a simple pleasure in years.

Dora's grin mimicked his own. "The only view I have is of the stars from my window." She waved toward an upper room in the vicarage where thin white-lace curtains sighed out with the dying breeze, then disappeared again from sight as if the house were drawing in a breath. "That's my room."

There was a long pause as William considered his abrupt feeling for Dora. It was not like Judy, he decided. It was not a love driven by sexual desire. His immediate thoughts of Dora consisted of wanting to protect and shelter her. His thoughts were interrupted by a voice.

"Dora, I hope you and William are gettin' along well," Father Donspy called, walking over to where they stood.

"Yes, Father. William has quite an exciting life in London."

"Indeed. He told me as much only this mornin'."

Dread wrapped clammy fingers around William's throat. Why on earth did he tell Father Donspy all that he did? William's face grew hot.

Donspy sensed his worry. "Yes, but never you mind that now. What I came over to tell you was the guest cottage has been made up for you. I thought I might take you that direction."

William looked around at the flint stone structure indicated. "That is very generous of you."

"Not after what you did today. You intervened for me and gave inspiration to these men that will last for months. Well done."

"Thank you," William replied.

Father Donspy showed him to the little cottage. It had only one room. Inside it was simple, but clean. There was a small table on the back wall, a cot, and a window facing the vicarage. Father Donspy wished him a good night and left William with a lantern.

Soon it grew dark outside. As William lay there thinking over the day, the only lights that could be seen anywhere were his lantern and one warmly glowing from the window of Dora's room.

William found a Bible near the bedside. He decided to read a few passages at random. By chance he turned to Proverbs 31. It spoke of a godly woman. About the only truly godly woman he had known was his mother. Certainly none of his pursuits were godly. It made him think of what he wanted more than anything in the world—a wife, and someday, a family.

For the first time in years, he prayed, thanking God for miraculously saving his life that day, for speaking to him in such a mysterious but real way. He prayed about his life, hoping he had not already lost any opportunity for someone as fine and gentle as Dora.

I am in awe of the way in which you move to execute your plan. Do something mighty for my mother's healing, I pray. Lead me to become a different man, and then, if it is possible, lead me to someone like Dora.

When he had said his amens, he blew out the light. A second after he did so, the light from Dora's window went out too. He wondered if perhaps she had been thinking of him, perhaps praying for him. He fell asleep then, thinking fond thoughts of home and even of his grandfather.

CHAPTER 10

Angelique sat in the corner of the garret room writing a letter to Albert on a scrap of paper she had borrowed from her friend Michelle. Throughout the house, other families murmured about the troubles of the day, taking comfort and reassurance in one another. The only comfort Angelique had was a fire crackling nearby and filling the tiny room with smoke. Her father was out for the day, drinking. But she had been avoiding her father as much as possible for the past month anyway, trying to keep her secret. But the sickness came more and more, and soon she knew it would be obvious to everyone what she was trying to hide.

She wrote:

> *Dearest Albert,*
> *I do not know if this letter will find you as I fear*
> *none of the others have, but I must try. The matter is*

the same: since you left I've noticed a change in my body, and it has become apparent to me that I am with child. Of course it is yours, and I know that you will return to me, my husband. But it must be soon, for I am growing daily and fear that I will no longer be able to conceal it from my father. You know what he would do since I have no document that will give our child your name.

You of course remember Madame Mannette. She has seen me every day and says that I . . . we are healthy, and I shall bear in the spring. The time will go too quickly, I fear, and when Father realizes, I will have no place to live. You must return soon, Albert. I long to see you and fear for your safety.

Despite the fear I feel, it is a beautiful thing. I am changing, almost growing with the child and feel. . .

Her writing came to an abrupt halt as her father stumbled through the door. She scrambled to hide the paper, but it was too late. Simon was wildly drunk and cursed as he saw her sitting on the floor.

"What is that, girl?" he bellowed, tromping across the floor toward her.

She would have moved away from his advance, but was trapped in the corner. "N-nothing, Father," she mumbled.

"Nothing? Then there is nothing to hide!" He lunged at her, tearing the paper from her grasp.

Angelique knew her father's reading was slow and took the time to move around him toward the door.

Each syllable Simon read aloud pierced Angelique's heart with fear.

"Father, please," she cried, "it's a letter to Albert."

"I can see that, girl. Now be still!" He continued reading. "The . . . mat-ter is. . ."

"Father!" she shouted over the words.

"I've noticed a . . . change in. . ."

Angelique rushed him, trying to pull the letter from his hands.

He caught her by the offending arm and held her fast as the dreaded words popped one at a time from his mouth. "I am with child." He mouthed the words again and Angelique was terrified as his grip tightened on her forearm and his face became red.

"Father, please," she pleaded again, "you must listen to me!"

Simon twisted her wrist backward until she knelt before him. His eyes seemed to flow hatred, his brows forming an arrow directed at her. He hissed at her with stale breath from the day's grog. "You whore!"

Tears flowed from her eyes, some from shame but most from the sharp pain in her arm.

Simon gripped harder, making her cry out. "To the bordello with you! Where you belong!" His volume rose on the last word echoing through the narrow house. He pushed her away and she fell, sobbing, to the floor.

"Oh, Father," she cried, trying to reach out to him, to plead with him. "He is my husband!"

His rage was not stayed by her comment. "By what law? You've had no wedding. No priest has sanctioned your union. Have I not taught you better than this?"

Angelique wished he would lower his voice. The other residents of the house were beginning to crowd around. She gazed at their faces, looking for sympathy. There was none.

"Answer me!" Simon grabbed her up by her hair. "How did I mislead you, to make you think. . ."

"We had no money to pay even the registrar. But Albert is my husband!" She struggled to free her hair from his hand and rose to her feet. "We've vowed our love by God himself." Some confidence returned to her voice as she explained.

Her father connected a sharp slap to her left cheek, and she fell again. He raged, "Blasphemous tart! The kind of vow every soldier makes to a foolish girl. He forgets his promises once he has what he wants and forgets her as well!"

"Not Albert! He is coming back for me!"

"And when is this hero returning to give your child a name?"

Angelique did not answer. She could not. Where was Albert? Why had he not answered her letters?

At the stricken look in her eyes, her father crowed, "I thought so. He has not written back. He is not coming back! Now get out!"

Angelique moved for the door. Lining the hallway were others who lived in the house. Some nodded, some shook their heads, but all wore a cold iron face of disapproval and disgust. Broken in spirit, Angelique fled into the street.

William marched the three dozen men of the Branson Fen militia down the long field and back at least twenty times a day for nearly a fortnight. Still it seemed they could not accomplish the simple task of walking in ranks without stumbling over the man in front or being tripped up by the man behind. Most had trouble keeping a steady pace so that the rows and columns were even and straight. Some men, more accurately half, could not remember their right foot from their left. As excited as they were about being military men, they were more like young puppies, stumbling over their own enthusiasm.

William was tired. It was the thirteenth day of

drilling. He had intended by then to have them well through half of Dundas's book of eighteen strategical maneuvers, but not these volunteers.

Finally, on that thirteenth day, William was fed up with the bumbling dust cloud that passed for a formation. He spotted two piles of fodder by a stone wall. This gave him an idea, and so he stopped the men. "Halt!" he ordered. After much staggering and a near fist fight, they jolted to a heaping stop.

They were a sorry-looking lot. All of them were bedraggled worse than the worn-out shoes on their feet. One of the men, Tim Corey by name, looked asleep where he stood. William walked over to Tim and clapped his hands next to Tim's ear, imitating the sharp report of a rifle cartridge.

Tim arched his back and tossed his head as if he were a gun-shy horse. He stumbled backward, tripping over his own feet before crashing to the earth like Swan's barn. The men were too tired to laugh.

"Wake up now!" William shouted.

Young Tim, around twenty-two years of age, scrambled to his feet in an instant.

William hovered over him for several seconds before pacing down the ranks. "Thirteen days we've practiced, four maneuvers we've studied, but none of you can

JAKE & LUKE THOENE

remember right from left!" He spun around and aimed his stern stare directly down an old man's throat.

"Me, sir?" the balding shovel-handle of a man said, swallowing hard and poking out his chin.

"Yes, you Private. How old are you?"

The man chewed and swallowed as if needing to digest the question. "They tell me I was born in the year that Queen Caroline died, your lordship. That'd make me two years shy of my threescore and ten."

"And. . ." William stopped in midthought. *Sixty-eight*, he thought. *How dreadfully old to be outside in the humid heat on a summer's midday. Why I'd have told a young whelp like me to kiss my big toe long since.*

He studied the ranks. All of the men looked to be in the same condition. It occurred to him that every man looked as if they would drop where they stood. William spoke softer and returned to Tim Corey. "Why are you so tired, Private?"

Tim replied carefully, "'Twas a late night last night, Cap'n. Me heifer givin' no consideration to the work I'd done already yesterday, which I didn't finish till after sundown, decided to calve last night, and didn't have the little one till well after sunup this morning. I do apologize for making such dreadful arsey-versy, but I must admit I haven't slept a wink in two days."

William was dumbfounded by the reality of the

man's speech. He felt almost like apologizing, in fact wanted to, but feared that might lead to disrespect for him among the ranks. "All right!" he yelled in his hard commanding tone. "You gentlemen see those piles of hay and straw over there?"

A sluggish reply followed. Most gazed without interest at the heaps of fodder. One was green and smelled refreshing. The other was brown and dry and had almost no smell at all. "We know what hay be, yer honor."

Ignoring the gibe, William said, "I want each of you to get a handful of straw, and stuff it in this boot!" William pulled a handful of the dry stocks from the pile and stuffed it under the laces of his right boot. "Like this!"

The volunteers crowded curiously around, hanging chins on each other's shoulders to see the oddity William was now performing.

"And I want you to take a portion of hay the same size and stuff it in your left boot, like this!"

The men rushed over to get a set of the freshly cut sprouts. After they had them securely laced in, each waited for further instruction, looking at William with baffled expressions. "What do you want we should do now, guvnor?" Tim inquired.

"Now, we march! Get back in ranks!" Responding

to the booming voice of command, the men did as they were told, though still confused.

William slapped his left leg and spoke slowly to them, as though they were three-year-olds. "Hay foot." He patted again, then slapped the other knee. "Straw foot."

They were still confused, but there was a spark of interest growing in their eyes.

William recited again in quicker order this time. "Hay foot, straw foot." He began to stamp each foot as he patted his leg. "Hay foot, straw foot, hay foot, straw foot."

Suddenly the men caught on and mimicked him perfectly. *How simple*, he complimented himself, *they've done this for a long time.* And soon the entire brigade was chanting, "Hay foot, straw foot, hay foot, straw foot," while stamping out some barbaric rhythm in the dirt.

"Good, good!" William bobbed his head to the rhythm. "You're catching on. Now let's try that in formation."

The men fell back into line, never stopping their chanting. Rounding up their attention with a wave of his hand, William started them on their march. "Hay foot, straw foot, hay foot, straw foot." They were getting the hang of things fast, William noticed.

There was a commotion in the back of the group,

and the ranks fell apart, circling around something. "It's Old Bryant!" someone yelled. "He's fallen!"

William hurried over and crowded through the barrier of bodies. There on the ground was Bryant, the elderly gentleman he'd scolded only minutes before.

Poor Bryant looked up at William. "I be all right," he said. "But my legs decided they was too tired to move and so with a mind of their own, decided to stop when the rest of me didn't."

A wave of embarrassment swept over William. Extending his hand to Bryant on the ground, he said, "I'm sorry, Bryant."

"Oh, never you mind, young buck," Bryant replied, accepting William's hand, which pulled him to his feet. "Us old'uns just gotta take it a bit slower."

All eyes were focused on William. It was enough for one day, William decided. "Company, dismissed," he said. A couple of the men went to escort Bryant up the hill toward his home. He must have felt ashamed he had fallen because he snapped at them both and went on alone.

William watched as the men crept up the long rolling hill, dragging their practice muskets: pitchforks, canes, and broomsticks, behind them. The whole experience gave William much to think about. These men were volunteers, not paid soldiers. They did not have money in their pockets, time to rest, or someone to take care of them while they drilled. Sure, he was tired, but he had nothing else to do during the day except train, while these men had families to support and work to accomplish. And the age of some of them was astounding. Old Bryant: sixty-eight. What the devil was he doing out here anyway? He should be home retired to a seat in his bit o'garden. Then the truth struck William even harder.

The reality was, these men were here to sacrifice their lives for their country. Their selflessness was astounding. William walked up the hill alone, pondering the concept.

Just as he was passing through the stone opening at the top of the hill, William spotted Dora. She was standing in the shade of an enormous oak tree and had been watching the drilling exercises. "Very impressive moves, Mr. Sutton." She smiled earnestly.

William felt his face grow doubly hot when he spotted her and reflected on the events of the day. "Oh, why yes, thanks." How long had she been standing there, he wondered. "Did you see the whole drill?" he asked, scratching between his shoulders nervously.

"Unfortunately, no. I've only just arrived, but made

it in time to see a real teacher improvising sponta-
neously."

"Why thank you, Miss Donspy. Really, it was nothing."

She walked alongside him. "That's what I think I
like most about you, William: your humble nature."

William ducked his head. No one had ever referred
to him as humble.

"I'm walking down to the shop to pick up the material for the men's uniforms. Would you care to accompany me?"

"It's in!" he exclaimed. "I'd be delighted to go."

They picked up the pace slightly. On the way Dora
told him a bit about the town's history and how the
Anglo-Saxons of the fen country had been the last hold-
outs against the Norman-French invaders back in the
last years of the eleventh century. "Father says that the
same spirit still exists here today."

"Your father is right," William agreed. He was
charmed to listen to Dora's lilting voice and her proud
chatter about her county, but part of his thoughts
returned again and again to the incident that afternoon.
Dedication, he reflected. *Selflessness is what is going to win
this war.*

Then they were at the shop. "Green!" William commented enthusiastically. "You picked forest green!"

Dora proudly lifted her brows, then nodded. "I know red is the color of England, and all the men wanted it, but when you said that many of the volunteer rifle companies wore green and since it seems to be the heritage of the sturdy yeoman and all that, we were sworn to get it."

"Well, this makes me so proud!" He took a bolt of cloth in his hands. "That you'd listen to me. That you'd pick green."

"I'll have to admit I also had to convince the ladies of the congregation."

The grin on William's face grew. "Oh, really? And what argument did you use?"

Dora cocked her head to one side. "I told them that our men deserve all the protection there is, and God made things on this earth different colors so that some would be noticed and so some would not. He also gave us a sense to imitate our surroundings if it means pro-tecting ourselves."

"Yes! Like a chameleon."

"What's that?"

"It's this really unusual reptile that I saw when I was on a voyage. It's a lizard that will change the color of its skin to whatever is nearest it when there is danger."

"A lizard?" she asked curiously, challenging the truth of William's story. "Change the color of its body?"

"Yes, really." He thought about how stupid it must have sounded. "I admit it was completely unbelievable until I saw it myself."

She smiled and walked out of the shop ahead of him.

William gazed around at everything. He was amazed at how much at home he felt in the village, even though he had been there only a short time.

His gaze took in the coaching hostel, the pub, and the public notice board in the town square. A new broadsheet was tacked up, and William sauntered over to inspect it. It was a recruiting poster.

Volunteers Wanted!
Notice is hereby given to all able-bodied men between the ages of sixteen and forty who are willing to serve His Majesty King George III on land and sea. For a short while recruits will be accepted in the newly forming regiment of the Royal Marines, known by all to be the finest fighting force in His Majesty's service. Persons willing to enjoin are entitled to present pay and good quarters, finest provender, and benefits to include prize money for captured vessels.

Come on, stout lads, ye hearts of oak. Is this not better than starving at home? Join in this campaign

against the evils of the tyrant Bonaparte. For with-
out, all shall surely be slaves.
God Save the King.

William noted that the date on which the recruiting officer would be in Branson Fen was only two weeks away, early in October.

Father Donspy stood beside a preoccupied William. The vicar, holding the reins of a tall bay mare, stopped without saying a word and gazed out at the militiamen, marching and countermarching in the lower pasture near the churchyard. He shielded his eyes from the low afternoon sun. "You've done well whippin' these men into shape, William."

William closed the cover of his silver pocketwatch and looked away from the glowing orange ball in the sky. "One minute fifty-nine," he said, following the men as they swiveled from two long rows and filed in pairs into a column. "They've worked very hard, Father, and it is fair to say, have improved dramatically."

Father Donspy patted him once on the back. "I think you're too modest. You have been a valuable addition to our community."

William watched as the men disappeared in the mist

that hung over the fen. Turning to Father Donspy he offered his sincere thanks.

Father Donspy interjected words that seemed to have been read from William's mind. "And it seems like only yesterday you were helpin' me with my horses and startin' a new life here."

William spoke not a word, only watched as a perfectly straight rank of men emerged from the fog.

"Are you sure you really need to be leavin'? We've all benefited from you so and . . . Dora will miss you."

The idea made William happy. He had spent so many brief but enjoyable little moments with her over the past weeks. He was fond of her. *What will I do when I am away and have only her memory?* he thought with pain. "She is a wonderful young lady, Father: respectable and kind, beautiful, yet innocent. She seems perfect in every way. I'm going to miss her as well."

Father Donspy grinned. "Aye, such perfection is rare. It seems she does take after her father." He chuckled.

William caught the glimmer in the vicar's eye. It was true: she did have a bit of her father's wit in her, and they seemed to share that same sparkle.

The two men laughed for several moments until the sound fell off. Then Donspy said, "The militia company will miss you as well. Duncan Harvey: How will he manage?"

Gesturing toward the tall man out in the field who was leading the group, William said confidently, "He'll manage, I'm sure of it. He'll drive them to perfection, wearing out the soles on their boots, long before the French come."

Three hundred yards away the men began their long march back up the hill. William grinned as each tipped his hat in tribute to Mr. Swan's fallen barn as they passed it.

"And what of these Royal Navy recruiters then? Shall they take you away tomorrow?"

"So the campaign poster read."

Father Donspy's voice sounded slightly mournful. "And will you be marched off to the coast to board some vessel immediately?"

"First thing."

"And there's nothin' you can do about it?"

"I'm afraid not," William responded sadly. "I've been paid my bounty moneys and have already spent half on new shoes, uniform, and coat. But it's not only that obligation that drives me to go. Since the day I met you, Father, my life has changed. I've become a new man, and since then God has created in me a conscience and a strong conviction that men out there who shall have far less in their lives than I've had already are willing to die to save us from the evil reign of Napoleon. What I have seen here—the willingness of these stout-hearts to work all day and then still come to drill when they have no illusions about what they will be facing should the invasion happen—they are the men of real valor, not me."

Father Donspy listened intently as William poured out his heart.

"My freedom, your freedom, England's freedom depends on it. Even the world's freedom is at stake. Old Boney will stop at nothing until he rules every man, woman, and child. Even in America he fights us through them. Holland has broken its pact with England. And the list goes on: Germany, Italy, Austria. It is truly a world war. Knowing what I know, feeling the way I now feel, it's not a passion for war or a need for an adventurous career that drives me to fight. It is knowing how I would feel if Britain lost the war while I did nothing."

Father Donspy reasoned with him. "But why the Royal Marines, my son? Certainly there are much safer corps to join at this time."

"Safer, yes," William interjected seriously. "But I am forced to ask my God where I am most needed. And he tells me, as is evident to all, the most immediate threat is the sea."

"Has God not brought you here to help us?" Donspy

argued. "Can you not see you are needed right here? Did God not specifically arrange for you to come here and complete this work?"

William had never felt the strength to stand up to Father Donspy, but now he was entirely too convicted to give in. "Out there across the Channel, a short cruise away, the French this very moment prepare for the invasion. That narrow space of water will shortly become the front line of battle on which, in consequence, the whole world will depend." He jabbed his finger eastward to emphasize his point. "Out there. Only miles away is where the real battle will be."

Lost for words, Father Donspy acquiesced. "I can't argue with your feelin's, William. And I certainly can't argue with God. If that's where he's tellin' you to go, you must go then. What I'm really tryin' to say in all of this is ... I will miss you too." Father Donspy reached out his arms to William. "You are family to us and to this town."

William was almost overwhelmed by his own emotions. After the loss of his family and life, to be accepted into someone else's family so unconditionally and now to be leaving was almost too much to bear.

He clasped Donspy tightly, speaking only the emotional words, "Thank you. Thank you for not mistrusting me, for giving me a chance to prove myself. You've given me new respect and a new life that no one can deny."

"Well, then." Donspy snuffled into a large pocket handkerchief. He mounted the bay. "Our men need rifles and London calls."

"I wish you could stay to see me off."

"Sorry, William." He laughed. "You remember the cannon. If anyone can talk the War Office out of some muskets it is I." Donspy backed the horse away.

"Cheers to that, Father. Safe journey, then."

"Godspeed to you."

William saluted him, and Father Donspy rode away. Reaching the top of the hill, the militiamen marched through an opening in the fieldstone wall where the rocks had tumbled down. William fell into line behind them.

"Gentlemen," William said in his parade-ground voice. "I give you a toast. Pray, raise your glasses." William's eyes were bright, and the resounding cheers were jolly.

The low-ceilinged, lantern-lit cellar seemed bright. The room was alive with men at five long tables, all resplendent in spanking-new green uniforms. One of them tipped his glass to William and said, "And to what shall we drink, Captain?"

William, rising to his feet, waved for attention. "This, my friends and comrades, represents something very special. More special than. . ."

Someone shouted, "Than Donspy's daughter?"

The men cheered. Duncan Harvey corrected, "Come now, William, there's naught more special than that!"

"All right! Enough of that, unless you want me to pour this port back into the bottle!" When the furor subsided he continued, "I was going to say, the toast is to something more special even than your new uniforms."

This remark set off a renewed round of cheering and the thumping of calloused fists on the plank table. When at last silence had been reestablished, all waited with patient smiles.

William held up his glass. "To the power of determined men! To the best militia force in England!"

"Hear! Hear!" they shouted in unison as they downed their drinks. Even the normally dour Lem, the sexton, was celebrating the work the men of his church had accomplished. He finished his glass, looked at it, and tilted it again to lick the two drops remaining.

Duncan Harvey stood and leaned over the table for the bottle. Filling the glasses of the men near him he said, "But the toasting is not complete without one more."

The men filled and lifted their glasses.

Harvey bobbed his head at William and blinked his eyes as he said, "To Captain William Sutton, the man who got us where we are today."

"Hear! Hear!"

"And who will lead us to glorious victory if the French should be so foolish as to attack!"

The room erupted into an overwhelmingly loud *hurrah*. "Three times three for William Sutton!"

Dora, entering the room with some of the other women to help clean up, stopped, gazing secretly at William from behind a brick pillar.

All drank but William. He waited until they had subsided before contradicting them sadly. "I'm sorry," he corrected. "I fear I cannot accept."

"What?" they all cried. "What do you mean?"

"I thank you, and I do pledge my heart to this village and its soldiers, but I'm afraid I must step down as captain."

Men watched and waited, glasses suspended in midair, hardly daring to breathe.

Lowering his glass, William explained. "I have to leave. I have joined the Royal Marines."

The news shocked Dora horribly. She threw her hands to her mouth and gasped. Her face was pale.

"I leave tomorrow," he continued. "But you are

crack troops, and I propose making Duncan Harvey your captain."

Duncan acted bashful, swaying. He cleared his throat and muttered, "Right, then, if there's no changin' hit."

"No," Dora whispered to herself. "You can't leave me."

"None whatsoever," William insisted. "And so I suggest a new toast: to Duncan Harvey, and his long career as your bold captain."

The toast was dutifully drunk, but the cheering was halfhearted at best.

Dora hurried from the room, tears streaming down her cheeks. William caught sight of this and watched her with dismay. As soon as he could, William bowed himself from the table and left in pursuit of her.

He searched the kitchen but found no sign of Dora. He searched the grounds and made his way through an opening in a high wall of bushes. There, underneath a great oak tree, on a quiet stone bench, she sat. Her face was in her hands, and she was sobbing. William rushed to her side.

"Dora, I'm sorry," he began. "You weren't meant to find out this way."

She lifted her head. She looked angry with him. "And when was I supposed to find out, then? After you'd left?"

"Dora, that's not fair. I intended to tell you privately, tonight."

"And since you are such a great one for plans, was it in your plans to make me love you and then leave this way?"

"No!" William was hurt. "Not at all. I feel—and have always felt. . ." He stopped to compose the lie. "From the first day I met you, I felt protective of you, as if you were my own sister."

This made her cry even harder. A dove in the tree echoed with a mournful cooing.

Earlier that day, William had felt so proud of his decision, so convicted that it was what God wanted, but now, seeing Dora this way made him feel miserable.

Dora stood and began to walk away.

"Wait, Dora," he called, chasing after her. He gently held her arm. "I wasn't being entirely truthful."

She looked up at him as if she were waiting to have her heart broken all over again, for him to say the words he hesitated to say.

"I care about you a lot."

A long pause followed as she searched his eyes. He knew she looked for the tiniest piece of dishonesty, but knew she would find none.

She blotted her tears with her apron. "I've never been in love before, William. I don't understand it. In spite of our short time together, no one has ever made me feel the way you do."

William listened in anguish, still resisting letting her know how strongly he really felt. It would only complicate matters and maybe, he thought, if he could somehow keep the truth from her, then he would be able to hide it from himself too.

"And now you say you are leaving . . . to go where?"

"A ship," he said simply.

"Some ship to set sail and probably sink out in the Channel somewhere, and I shall never see you again."

"No, no, no," he corrected. "If you will permit it, I will call on you when I return."

Several leaves fell from the oak, drifting downward like the sands of earth's hourglass. William thought about the season and how Napoleon's British campaign must happen soon. His thoughts betrayed him.

"No, William," Dora said firmly. "You'll not do this to me. I will give my love to no man who will not share his with me." She ripped herself loose from his arms and ran off sobbing into the night.

William sat down on the bench. It had gone so terribly badly. He looked up at the moon. It was extremely bright, causing the passing clouds to fall into shadow as they were illuminated from behind. He thought about Dora and her purity of soul. She was like the moon when compared to every other woman—Judy and the rest. Even the brightest cloud turns gray when it passes near the moon.

His head falling into his hands, William rubbed his face, determined to dismiss Dora from his mind. Gritting his teeth, William threw his head back as he jumped to his feet, fists clenched. He decided to leave that very night.

William scrambled aboard the three-masted frigate at Portsmouth Harbor. While being rowed across the harbor in his uncomfortably scratchy new red uniform jacket, he studied the name *Pegasus* engraved on a wooden sign mounted just below the poop deck. Boarding a ship for the first time since the fire, William could not help but be reminded of the dreadful night when he lost the *Stronghold*, and his life began to unravel.

The decks were covered with men completing various tasks from holystoning the planks to stretching new canvas and tightening the rigging. He followed more than two dozen Royal Marines below. Quarters were tight in the middle deck. Each man was allotted scarcely twenty-two inches of width in which to hang his hammock. William stowed his bag of belongings beside a cannon, over which he would sleep that night.

There were more than forty other marines on board. The captain, two lieutenants, two sergeants, and two corporals made up the officers. The rest were privates.

Counting the captain, his lieutenants, the warrant and petty officers, idlers like the carpenter and sailmaker, and the ordinary seamen, called *ratings*, combined with the marines, there were one hundred and eighty in all, making this a comparatively small crew for a warship. Operation and guard of the ship were divided into port and starboard watches in four-hour shifts.

Six bells rang, signaling eleven in the morning. William heard the trill of the bosun's whistle, piping for all hands aft. William's contingent of marines had arrived just in time to witness punishment.

William stood stiffly at attention in a file of a dozen marines stretching across the poop deck. His black leather hat perched correctly atop his head and his sword belts formed a perfect X on his chest. His musket, bayonet fixed in place, was at his left side.

On the quarterdeck, just below the rank of marines, a sailor was tied to a wooden grate, sentenced to thirty lashes for an extremely tardy return from shore leave. After sentence was read, the drummer began a steady roll on his instrument.

The bosun's mate stretched out the cat, letting any

tangles in the cords unsnarl, before bringing it whistling forward to lash the prisoner's shoulders. After the tenth stroke, the man screamed with every lash received, though William considered him lucky. A man could be condemned to as many as twelve hundred lashes.

When the man was cut down and hauled off to sick bay, Captain O'Brian read the Articles of War, addressing the men about proper behavior. It seemed all had heard it before, though the severity of the consequences made everyone appear attentive. "Fleeing in battle, punishable by death. Murder, punishable by death. Desertion from His Majesty's ship, punishable by death . . . punishable by death . . . punishable by death."

As one of the recent recruits, William knew no one and because of this spoke very little. As soon as his gear was stowed and some last-minute supplies were brought aboard, the bosun piped all hands to stations, and the order was given to weigh anchor. William was sent below to help man the capstan, a huge winch used for hauling up the great weight of anchor and cable. Long timbers slipped into square-notched holes provided levers for many men to push against, walking around and around.

William had only just started pushing when he heard a familiar voice shouting, "Heave! Get your backs into it!" He glanced over his shoulder and spotted

Thomas dressed in red tailcoat and bicorne hat to prove he was a lieutenant. William's spirits jumped. It would not be such a solemn cruise after all. Thinking it unwise to break ranks, even to acknowledge his closest friend in the world, William continued to push.

Thomas was visually sweeping the room when William rounded the other side of the drum of the capstan, coming face-to-face with him. Thomas glanced past, at first not noticing, then whipped his head back. "William, my friend!" he involuntarily called.

Everyone turned at once to see what man could have possibly drawn the lieutenant's attention. Thomas cleared his throat and stiffened his back. "Back to work, men," he ordered. "Private Sutton. Come here, if you please."

William fell out of line. He was overjoyed to see Thomas for the first time since the cottage. The month gone by had not been that long, but William had changed so dramatically that Thomas hardly recognized him, clean-shaven and in uniform. For his part, William hardly knew where to begin.

He saluted. "Lieutenant. What can I do for you?"

"Private Sutton, you will report to officer's quarters directly upon the anchor being catted and all secure."

"Aye, aye, sir," William responded, and after the

anchor was retrieved and fastened to the beam called a *cat*, he made his way aft.

It was but a few minutes later when Thomas entered the room. "My good man! William, how are you?" He reached out his hand and gave William a hearty handshake.

Not wanting to endanger the discipline due to Thomas or to make his messmates think he was after special treatment, William continued to address Thomas formally. "I'm fine, sir. I have been through a great many changes, as you may have guessed."

Thomas stood back to examine his friend. "I can see," he said, holding up both hands. "And to find you here. It's just such a great surprise."

William nodded. "It is for me too."

They talked a few minutes, catching each other up on the latest details. William explained his experience on the road, how he had met Father Donspy and trained the volunteer group, then about his being convicted to join the marines. He also briefly spoke about Dora and what a wonder she was.

Thomas told William of the most amazing battle where they had come between two French seventy-fours. Grappling hooks were thrown over, securing one, the *St. Nazaire*, to the *Pegasus*. Since they were so close, the other French warship, the *Toulon*, had to then cease firing. Fortunately, the wind died away, leaving the second vessel unable to aid the first.

Within ten minutes of being boarded, the French had struck their colors, and the British then turned the guns of both ships on the *Toulon*, which had promptly fled.

William shook his head with amazed disbelief. "Captain O'Brian's hungry for blood and prize money then, is he?"

"I'd agree with you fully. We took in more than sixty thousand pounds for the *St. Nazaire* and her contents."

"Sixty thousand pounds!" William exclaimed. "Captured the ship and the entire Bank of France, it sounds like. What was your share?"

Thomas grinned and burst into laughter. "Fifty pounds!"

"And what of Boney?" William inquired.

Thomas looked around before replying. "It's just scuttlebutt, you understand, but there is word that Napoleon has given his admiral, Villeneuve, an ultimatum: sail, or be broken and replaced. We may see action soon!"

Just then the bosun called all hands to make sail, and in another moment the *Pegasus* leaned into her starboard tack. The voyage was under way.

CHAPTER 11

Knowing that Napoleon was preoccupied with the invasion of England, Austria and Russia recognized an opportunity. In September their combined forces were sent against the emperor's extreme eastern flank, invading Bavaria in the southern German states. Their massed soldiers totaled close to three hundred thousand men, enough to give them nearly a two-to-one superiority over the French.

Such was the discipline and organization of Napoleon's troops that they could leave garrison duty in Boulogne and cover five hundred miles of terrain in little more than two weeks. As the advance guard, the cavalry of the Grande Armée reached the Danube before their Austrian opponents even suspected them of having crossed the Rhine.

Facing the troopers of the First Hussars and the rest

of the mounted French force totaling ten thousand were fifty thousand men commanded by the Austrian Archduke Ferdinand. His headquarters were in Ulm, across the valley of the Neckar River.

It was Albert's good fortune to have drawn duty as a staff aide-de-camp on the day before battle was expected. As such he was posted to Marshal Joachim Murat's headquarters in order to carry orders back to the regiment when the battleplan had been decided.

He was in Murat's tent when the conference with generals Walther and Kellermann took place. It was not his place to speak, but in such a close space Albert could not help overhearing what passed in the discussion.

"It is the will of the emperor that we make an assault on the enemy tomorrow at dawn," Murat said. "We are to keep in close contact all day, thus convincing the Austrians that the main attack will come from the west side of the valley."

"When in reality . . . ," Kellermann questioned.

"In reality, all of First Corps and Third Corps will bypass the valley on the north, turning south beyond Ulm, and thus. . ."

"Getting between the archduke and his Russian reinforcements," concluded Walther.

Murat's mass of curly hair merged with his brushy sidewhiskers. "It is the emperor's plan to then attack the

Austrians from the east, disposing of them before their other forces can intervene. As you can see, gentlemen, it is essential that we make our demonstration last the entire day, in order to be convincing and prevent the archduke from readjusting his line to meet the real threat from the rear. I think that summarizes our needs. Till tomorrow then." The generals took their leave of the marshal, but Albert remained to receive orders.

Hastily writing with a quill pen, Murat took time to raise his eyes from his work to study Albert. "You are young to already possess the Legion of Honor," he remarked, gesturing at the medal on Albert's chest. "How did you come by it?"

Albert related the battle of Petit Port, modestly downplaying his own role in the action.

"Ah," Murat exclaimed. "The emperor made special note of you. He said you spurned his offer of an artillery appointment in favor of the cavalry."

"I am sorry if I disappointed his majesty," Albert replied with chagrin.

"No, no," Murat retorted. "The artillery is a place for clerks and men of science, not for dashing young fellows like yourself. I understand you come from the Left Bank—a penniless student, no doubt. Nothing to be ashamed of, that. I myself am from a poor family. In fact

I came up through the ranks to be a marshal of France, so you see how rewarding the cavalry can be."

Albert wondered if Murat's successes might also owe something to his position as the emperor's brother-in-law, but he carefully kept even his face from whispering such a thought. Besides, despite Murat's flamboyant taste in extravagant uniforms, he was regarded by the cavalry as personally courageous.

Murat signed his name to the orders, authenticated them with sealing wax and a signet ring, and passed the document to Albert. "I will pay particular attention to you in tomorrow's engagement," he said. "You are dismissed."

Albert groaned to himself as he mounted Balthasar. "I offended the emperor, and now I am to be under the watchful eye of the marshal of all the Imperial cavalry! What about just doing my duty as a good soldier?"

The next day Albert drew himself up in Balthasar's saddle and stretched to his full height in the stirrups, wincing as he did so. It was a futile attempt to see through the almost unbreathable pall of smoke and thick fog that completely filled the Neckar river valley.

The bowl just east of the French position reverberated with the steady, deep-voiced thumping of the Austrian artillery. Since before dawn the enemy cannon, planted firmly atop the heights only three miles away, had been pummeling the valley floor. The bombardment had been so persistent and the chest-fluttering pulses of exploding shells so constant that any lull in the firing made Albert wonder if his heart had stopped beating.

Colonel Rouvillois assured the First that everything was proceeding according to plan. "This incessant firing at nothing means the Austrians still think of us as the main front," he said. "But I have just received word the main body of the Grande Armée is directly north and beginning the envelopment, so it is now that we must redouble our efforts to make the deception complete."

How like an officer, Albert thought. *He begins by telling us how well we have done and concludes by saying nevertheless, we must do it harder!*

Since early morning, successive waves of hussars, chausseurs, cuirassiers, and dragoons had dared the artillery barrage, galloped their mounts into the corridor of grapeshot, shrapnel, and musketfire, and galloped out again. Not all returned, of course. The First was lucky: only three troopers were killed, six wounded, and ten horses shot from under.

Albert himself had been struck by a shell fragment. After cutting Balthasar's bridle it had then sliced into the leather of his boot, nicking his ankle with a minor wound that nevertheless filled his footgear with blood.

And now it was time for the First to ride forward and harass the enemy again. Cyrus was overjoyed, even as he watched an exhausted column of dragoons streaming back from the front. "Ha!" he said. "I was afraid that the dragoons would actually break the Austrian line before we got another crack at them. Today is my day to achieve something great; I feel it."

Albert was too tired to remind Cyrus that no one expected to break the Austrian line and that living through the campaign should be heroic enough. But there was no arguing with Cyrus when he was in his glory-minded mode.

"The First will advance," Colonel Rouvillois ordered, and the troop started forward at the walk. They remained in columns of two until they reached the bottom of the slope just beyond the range of the Austrian shelling. There they wheeled into battle order: two lines of fifty mounted men. Albert and Cyrus were at the extreme right end of the second rank. Beyond them was Corporal Fosse. Past him were only oak trees and the valley stretching up toward the Alps.

For Albert the hardest part of any advance was the walk-trot-canter sequence that carried the regiment into the descending shells. Since the pistol he carried in his right hand would draw no blood unless fired from fifty paces or less, it was a long time before the First could pay back the Austrians for the blows they were receiving.

A shell exploded between the ranks, blowing two troopers out of the saddle and disemboweling their mounts. Another burst in the air ahead of the front rank and three more riders tumbled into the cold, much-churned mud. Above them on the Austrian-held incline, trumpets rang out. Suddenly the tempo of cannonfire increased and rifle bullets zipped and sung in the air like swarms of angry bees.

Then Albert was under the rain of death and charging at full gallop up the slope. His saber dangled from the sword knot on his right wrist, and he involuntarily held it farther from his side so that the jolting ride would not cause the blade to strike Balthasar in the flanks.

Cyrus was a full length ahead. He turned about in his saddle, grinning wildly, shouting and waving his pistol for Albert to "Come on! Come ON!"

A swirl of wind parted the smoke. Just ahead, another hundred yards away, was a line of Austrian infantry in green-and-white uniforms. Even as Albert saw them, they disappeared again in a cloud of smoke as they fired a massed volley of muskets.

A hussar trumpet ordered the front rank to wheel to the left, the second to the right, doubling again the length of the attacking line. *Good*, Albert thought, *it is almost over now. We will sweep up to clash and then withdraw.*

A tree stump, splintered and riddled with bullets, loomed up. Albert set his spurs, and Balthasar cleared the low obstruction, barely missing the body of a soldier killed in an earlier attack. His uniform was so muddy and bloodstained that Albert could not tell to which side he belonged. Then a rifle ball whistled past his ear, and he cocked the hammer on the pistol.

Twenty paces ahead a man in green drew his musket up to his shoulder. Albert flung himself across Balthasar's neck, heard the report of the rifle, then presented the pistol and fired. The Austrian clutched his arm and dropped the musket.

Transferring the now-empty pistol to his rein hand, Albert grasped the hilt of the saber and swung it around his head. Beside him Cyrus was going through exactly the same motions as the First Hussars clattered into the front rank of enemy soldiers.

A man jabbed at Albert with a bayonet. Albert parried the thrust with a backhanded stroke, then flipped the tip of the blade around to catch the enemy soldier in the cheek. Without even looking at the result, Albert hastily slashed hard across his body at an officer who aimed a sword blow at Balthasar's head. Metal rang against metal, and then Cyrus rode over the top of the Austrian, whooping like a madman and still yelling, "Come on!"

Albert heard Cyrus grunt. It was not a cry of pain or a scream, just a low exclamation of surprise, as if his friend had been struck in the stomach by a fist. Behind the First a trumpet sounded recall. The other trumpets picked up and repeated the order. The mission was accomplished, the harassment complete. Time to recross the killing zone of shellfire and regroup.

But Cyrus seemed not to have heard the trumpet call. He spurred his black horse into the second rank of the enemy, slashing right and left. Ahead was an Austrian battle flag, green with a gold eagle, fluttering at the end of a spiked pole. With Albert yelling, "Recall, Cyrus! Come back!" Cyrus jumped his mount over a fallen heap of men, knocked aside a sergeant major, slashed at a captain and seized the standard. He waved it wildly around his head as Albert spurred up alongside him, hacking his way beyond four more assailants and getting a musketball through the top of his shako.

"Recall, Cyrus!" Albert repeated, pointing with his sword back down the slope.

Cyrus nodded. His smile was gone, and in its place was a curious, tight-lipped grimace.

Halfway back down the incline into the concealing mist, Cyrus's horse stumbled, then buckled on both front legs. Cyrus scrambled awkwardly out of the saddle, still clutching the captured banner. He reached up toward Albert for an arm to help him up. "My horse has been hit," he observed unnecessarily. Then as he mounted behind Albert, "And so . . . have I."

Balthasar carried the two men back out of the skirmish. The artillery fire was less on the return, as if the Austrians were also tired of the battle and willing to stop for breath. "I . . . told you," Cyrus said heavily, "this was my day." This phrase he repeated several more times, his voice growing ever more faint.

By the time Balthasar trotted into the French lines, Cyrus was not speaking at all. When Albert reined to a halt, Cyrus fell off onto the ground, dead. The captured standard had to be pried from his fingers.

Albert's squadron made camp in a two-room stone farmhouse standing on a rise that overlooked the distant battlefield. A pall of dense smoke hung over the Neckar river valley like an unnatural mist shrouding the dead and dying of both armies. After the ear-shattering sound of the cannonade the quiet seemed thick and palpable, as though the absence of sound were itself deafening. The sky grew darker as storm clouds drifted in from the east. Drops of heavy rain fell in intervals, adding to the dense and humid atmosphere.

In spite of the victory the bivouac was a sad one. A solitary candle lit the interior of the farmhouse where Albert sat moodily with a half-dozen other troopers. Without the swagger and bravado of Cyrus, the little company was subdued and gloomy. Albert's sky-blue tunic, stained with Cyrus's blood, was unbuttoned. Braided earlocks damp with sweat clung to his mud-spattered cheeks. The captured flag was propped, unregarded, in a corner.

Henri Bonard, the five-year-veteran of the First Hussars, entered the silent enclave, ran his thumbnail across his thick moustache, and glared scornfully at Albert. With his index finger he flicked Albert's sidelock.

"Mourning our dead? You have the look of a drowned cat, Penfeld. Here! Look at me." Henri indicated his surprisingly immaculate appearance.

Albert remarked bitterly, "You put us all to shame."

"And you put our fallen comrades to shame. Cyrus's spirit is but a little way above us, taunting the English dead, no doubt."

"Not taunting, I think." Albert did not look up to meet the challenge.

"What then? Asking their pardon for killing them?"

"In death all men, English or French, find themselves common ground."

Henri laughed. "Dust to dust. A grave discussion. Well spoken! Enemies in life, brothers in death. Indeed! So what is the use of sadness for those of us who live? We make the English die first. That is the point of the contest, hein?" He pulled a flask of brandy from his boot and uncorked it. Drawing a long swig he passed the container to Albert who gratefully accepted, drank, then passed it on.

Henri, suddenly jolly, sank down beside Albert, nudging him on the shoulder. "Confess it: you have always wanted to know how I keep my earlocks straight."

Albert smiled ruefully. The absurdity of such a topic after a day of killing almost made him laugh.

Encouraged, Henri held up a braid. "You have won the right to hear my secret. You see, I've woven a pistol ball into it for weight. So it hangs with dignity no matter what the weather or situation."

"And how do you keep your tunic so clean in a battle?" asked a drowsy trooper from the corner.

"I do not let the cursed English any closer than the point of my saber."

Henri Bonard attempted to fill the gap left by Cyrus with his bluster. Two more flasks of brandy surfaced and floated around the little room and toasts were drunk to the victory. Beneath the roll of laughter and the jokes that followed, Albert's mind remained fixed on how impossibly lonely he would be now that Cyrus was gone and then turned to Angelique.

"*Diable!*" he heard Bonard exclaim from the guard shack. "You will never guess what has arrived."

"Champagne?" someone ventured.

"Orders sending us back to Paris for a month?"

"Better!" Bonard countered. "Mail!"

There was a general exclamation of approval at this announcement. Since the rapid redeployment to the Austrian front, there had been no mail for the regiment. Then, today of all days, it caught up with them.

Bonard refused to relinquish his grip on the leather pouch, doing all the sorting himself and making obscene comments about the probable contents of each missive. "Here's one from your wife, Drouot," he said. "She tells you she is pregnant again. Let's see, how long have you been away? Eleven months?"

Albert winced, shut his eyes, and did his best to shut his ears as he curled into a ball and attempted to sleep.

"One for Cyrus," Bonard hummed to himself. "What shall we do with it? Auction it? It appears to be perfumed."

The comment "Send it to the dead letter office" was hissed down.

"Look here, Penfeld," Bonard noted, nudging Albert with the toe of his boot. "There's even one for you. Your parole is up, and they want you back in prison. See, it is marked from the Brest Prefecture of Police."

Grabbing the envelope from Bonard's hands, Albert tore it open. The Brest police knew perfectly well of the smuggler, Francois D'Chiminee, the note said. It gave an address where he could be contacted and further suggested that if Colonel Rouvillois of the First Hussars wished the scoundrel arrested, the gendarmes would be pleased to oblige.

As if taking his cue from the letter, Rouvillois himself strode into the room, and the tired troopers rose and stood stiffly at attention. "A good day's work, eh, men?" he said. "Penfeld, you are to be honored for your part in the capture of the Austrian standard. On the morrow you are detached for service to the Imperial staff. Your new duties will be explained to you then. Carry on."

CHAPTER 12

———⚬———

Balthasar's hooves thundered rhythmically on the dirt road to Paris. Though he felt like no kind of hero for having returned both Cyrus's body and the captured Austrian flag, he was, nevertheless, treated as one.

His Legion of Honor medal was garnished with an encircling band of jeweled laurels, and he was detached from the First Hussars and made a special aide-de-camp to the emperor's staff.

His first assignment was to carry a set of sealed orders from Napoleon to Admiral Villeneuve of the French fleet. Since if he was in danger of being captured the secret orders would have to be destroyed, Albert was also entrusted with knowing their contents.

The emperor was decidedly not pleased with Villeneuve's lack of aggression toward the British. He was being relieved of command. His replacement was ordered to move the combined fleet into Mediterranean waters, there to wait the following spring and another attempt to mount the cross-Channel invasion.

Albert was to seek Villeneuve in the port of Brest, but if the admiral was not there, to pursue him by ship if necessary. It was expected that Albert's route from the battlefields of Austria to the seacoast at Brest would carry him through Paris. How curious, Albert thought, that now he had both personal and military business to take him to Brest.

So it was that Albert's mind was not on soldiering. The trip to Paris was important to him for only one reason. He could finally see Angelique, hold her, and tell her how much he loved her. What would be the first thing to say to her, he wondered. And she to him?

His heart rose as he cantered along the river, past the Rue St. Jacques and the turn that would have taken him straight to Angelique. *So close*, he thought. It seemed the only disappointment he had that day was that he was expected at the Tuileries very early. He would have to wait to see Angelique until after the business was finished.

Entering the city, he reigned Balthasar to a stop and patted him on the shoulder. The emperor's residence and offices were in the Tuileries palace, originally built for Catherine de Médicis in 1563. Since Napoleon was in Austria at the head of his troops, Albert was to see Marshal Berthier, minister-of-war and chief of the Imperial staff. Albert was instructed to inform Berthier of the change in admirals, and in turn Berthier was authorized to provide Albert with any money and travel permits needed for him to complete his mission.

Outside the heavy wooden doors were four sentries from the Imperial Guard. Napoleon had personally selected them for their fierceness in battle. Guardsmen had to be six feet tall, have served ten years with the army, and must have performed heroically in at least three campaigns. They were widely regarded for their personal loyalty to the emperor and for the facial hair that provided their nickname: Old Moustaches. Dressed in large bearskin bonnets and sporting ferocious expressions, they scowled suspiciously at Albert as he entered. Every one, Albert noted, was missing a limb or an eye; otherwise they would have been in Austria with the rest.

Albert paid them no heed as he entered the hall. Inside he was greeted by an officer who led him up a flight of stairs and into a long marble corridor that echoed with the whispers of worried men. In a room off the corridor, a hundred and fifty uniformed men milled and mumbled, most already holding official envelopes in their hands.

To Albert's surprise, his orders, emblazoned with the

personal seal of the emperor, carried him past the crowd to the head of the line and on into Berthier's office. Marshal Berthier, whom Albert had seen in Boulogne, was open and friendly in contrast to the expressions worn by the guardsmen. "So, young cavalry trooper, we meet again," he said. The marshal dismissed his aide, then opened the communiqué and studied it without speaking. "Do you know what this contains?" he asked with a frown.

"*Oui*, monsieur," Albert asserted. "Is it in order?"

Berthier frowned again. "Yes and no. Admiral Villeneuve, fearful of being relieved from command, has moved his fleet at last. He successfully slipped into the Spanish harbor at Cadíz."

"Spain," Albert murmured. "So far."

The chief-of-staff reexamined the document. "But his highness allows no argument. Villeneuve is relieved and must be informed. You will continue to Brest as planned, but you must take ship immediately for Spain."

"Your pardon, Marshal," Albert said. "I have just this day ridden in from the front. I thought perhaps. . ."

"Of course." Berthier smiled. "You are not expected to continue your mission until tomorrow. See my aide to draw some funds. He will arrange for your accommodations as well."

"Respectfully, Marshal," Albert corrected, "the funds

will be most welcome, but my accommodations are already provided for."

"Very well," Berthier replied, standing to receive Albert's parting salute. "Remember, Penfeld: stress to Villeneuve that above all else, he must do *nothing* to endanger the fleet!"

From his perch atop Balthasar Albert saw the commotion in front of Angelique's house before he reached it. Five soldiers wrestled with someone who kicked and flailed on the ground. The men were of the gendarmerie, most likely sent to collect and imprison a dissident. Napoleon did not like people speaking out against him, no matter how uninfluential or unimportant they might be.

Albert's heart dropped. Could it be they had finally arrested Angelique's father, Simon? Albert smiled slightly as two of the officers flew backward in tandem like an acrobatic act. "Not doing a very good job of it," Albert mumbled. He caught sight of Simon as they finally brought him under control. His face was beet-red, and he screamed obscenities about the men, their ancestry, and Napoleon himself. Then he stopped struggling when he saw Albert.

Peering up out of his battered face, one eye swollen shut and the other bleeding profusely, he was still able to identify Albert at once. "You!" he screamed. "You've done this to me. I swear I'll kill you, boy."

"No, monsieur," Albert returned. "You have brought this upon yourself."

The soldiers hoisted Simon upright as he spat toward Albert. The butt of one musket came down hard on Simon's head, and he cried out in pain.

"No!" Albert yelled at the soldier. "He is drunk, you see? It is not necessary to subdue him further."

"Mind your own business," the gendarme retorted. "He has cost me two of my best men, one with a broken jaw. Do not interfere, or we will be forced to arrest you as well!" Then the officer returned to clamping on a set of twenty-pound leg irons.

"Monsieur Simon!" Albert called after him as he was dumped into a featureless black carriage. "Where is Angelique?"

Simon's face appeared at the square of barred grating in the door. The one word he spoke nearly felled Albert from his saddle. "Dead!"

The image of Simon's glistening, bared teeth and bloody, raging countenance burned into Albert's eyes as the dreadful, fatal word echoed and reechoed in his ears.

Albert stabled Balthasar at the tavern known as *Salle Des Pas Perdus*, the Hall of Lost Footsteps. How appropriate the name seemed for this hour of his life. With Heloise's dying words he had lost his identity. Now Angelique was forever beyond his reach. There was no familiar path left for him to follow.

Alone at a table in the corner of the squalid room he brooded and drank in hopes of dulling the agony of his loneliness. Like a wanderer lost in a dark forest he waited for some light of understanding to lead him home, but none appeared.

It was past ten o'clock when he staggered out drunk onto Place St. Michel. A heavy rain fell, washing the streets and the fetid air. Albert gulped the air like a man who had been held underwater. Groping along the rough plaster of the buildings he turned onto Rue St. Severin and spotted a glimmer of candlelight emanating from the windows of the Church of St. Severin. Here was a familiar place. As a child Albert had been drawn to it. The great doors were covered with horseshoes brought by medieval knights as votive offerings when they were about to start on a long journey. The priest, it was said, had heated the key of the church in the incense lamp and then branded the horse on the flank as a symbol of blessing to guide the knight's footsteps home again after battle.

The memory of his boyish delight in the tale struck Albert like a sword. He knew the truth of war now. He understood the finality of death; the chasm left when love was gone.

With a cry of anguish, he stumbled toward the ancient building, past the well where seven centuries of pilgrims stopped to drink, and burst through the iron-shod doors and into the foyer.

He glanced around in the dim light. The steel-colored stone walls seemed to weep moisture from the downpour outside. He kicked the door shut behind him. A blast of cold air followed, causing the candles at the altar to flicker.

The sanctuary was nearly empty. One young man, dressed in the robes of a student at the Sorbonne, prayed in silence in a side chapel. Father Julien, a grizzled old priest who had survived the Terror and escaped the guillotine by fleeing to Ireland, now lovingly dusted the worn oak pulpit with an oily rag.

Reeking of cheap wine, Albert exhaled a silent belch and staggered forward. A flask held one remaining swallow, which he gulped down. Swaying awkwardly in the aisle he shook the container above his mouth for the last drops. Albert placed the empty vessel on the base of a pillar, then watched as it teetered and fell, echoing loudly in the building. Wiping his mouth with one hand and steadying himself with the other he made his way toward the confessional booth at the back of the chapel.

Pausing from his work, Father Julien raised his eyes to meet Albert's. Albert gazed for a moment at the tall, lean cleric. What a friend Father Julien had been in Albert's youth. The church had supported Heloise with food and friendship as she had fought to raise a young boy in a difficult time. Father Julien had educated Albert and a handful of other children when there had been no other school.

Albert grinned and waved at the priest, then bowed drunkenly and dived into the confessional.

Julien was moved with pity. "So the prodigal is come home," he murmured, raising his eyes briefly to the crucifix and the long-suffering Christ upon it. With a shrug he joined Albert in the booth. "Welcome home, Albert. We missed you at Heloise's funeral."

"Bless me, Father, for I have. . ." Albert did not know why he had come or what he was doing here. Had he come to confess his sins out of old habit? With a spinning head braced in his trembling, cold hands, Albert thought back through the progression of this long and terrible day. "My God. . . ." Albert groaned.

"He hears you."

Albert began to laugh, and the sound of it was frightening to him. He fought to control himself. "Hears me? Like he hears the groans of men dying on the battlefield? There is no God! Were there a God, there would be no evil."

"He hears the living and the dying alike."

"And when the cannon roars and men cry out in terror at the vision of their own death? The Englishman and the French patriot each call out to their God to save them, to win the battle! Who does God fight for then? The French or English?"

"He fights for the soul of every man. French and English. Sometimes he wins. Sometimes he does not."

"He has lost the battle for my soul," Albert said bitterly. "First Heloise, and then when Angelique died."

"Angelique? Who has told you this?"

Tears rolled from Albert's eyes, and he choked on the words. "Her father told me today."

"Albert," spoke Father Julien softly, "Angelique still lives in the . . ."

"Kingdom of heaven? With Heloise? With my true mother, whoever she may have been? They are all dead, just dead, and I am alone. Heaven is an illusion. And my life has been lived in illusion and lies. You knew the truth of who I am, who I am not, and did not tell me," Albert yelled and stormed from the cubicle.

"If these are your reasons for denying Christ," Father Julien said, emerging after him, "then you are an amateur atheist, boy. These are the facts of who you are.

From the first day you were brought to her—hungry, squawking, pitiful—Heloise Penfeld offered you to God. She knew it was a miracle that you had come to her. An answer to her lonely prayer. You brought her heaven's love and joy as surely as if the Archangel Gabriel had delivered you to her doorstep. So? God brought you by way of a smuggler who found you ... somewhere. I am not clear on that part of it. But you are God's child, I do not doubt. The love you brought with you is proof of that. The fact that you survived is proof. There is one truly faithful heart in all the universe and that is the heart of Christ. He owes allegiance to no nation, but cares only for the soul of each individual. For you, Albert. And yet you cannot see God with your eyes, so you deny he exists. Things are unhappy for you, so you deny the faith you held so firmly as a child."

"It was easy to believe when I was a child."

"How many stars are in the skies, Albert?"

"How could I know that?"

"'Prove you exist,' you demand of the Almighty! *Mon Dieu!* I say to you, Albert, prove to me that God does not exist! If you cannot, then tremble in your arrogance! You would have to be God yourself and search the universe in order to know with certainty that heaven does not exist! You cannot even count the stars. Are you God? No! Arrogance. You accept your despair

219

and doubt as backhanded proof that God does not exist. But God's love preserved your life and brought you to Heloise. And nothing can separate you from your Father's love, not even your loneliness and denial." The good priest's fierceness softened then. "Now on to other matters. Albert, I think I can renew your faith."

"Renew? I never had any." Albert turned toward the doors, but the priest caught him by the arm.

"The battle for your soul is not finished, but first there is a truth I must show you. Come with me," Father Julien instructed.

The two walked side by side into the chapel.

"What would it take," the priest whispered, "to make you believe?"

"Give me back my life, Father Julien," Albert replied. "Can you do that?"

"And of what does your life consist?"

"My love. Angelique."

"You should know that only God himself can perform a miracle of such magnitude, as Lazarus was so blessed."

"Which is why I will not believe. There never was one so deserving of life as Angelique."

"Perhaps you should have told her that. And perhaps you still can. I think your anger is not with God but with yourself for denying her."

"You knew of that?"

Father Julien clasped him on the shoulder. "We had many talks about you . . . and the baby."

Albert grimaced. Tears splashed on the cold floor as he contemplated the life he could have had with his family.

The priest took Albert's chin in his hand and lifted his head. "The way to come to peace with yourself is to tell Angelique now. All you should have told her while she was alive. You denied her a proper marriage and because of that her father cast her out. Do not deny your penance now."

Albert fell hard to his knees at the altar. He whispered fiercely, "God, if you are there, tell Angelique. Forgive me. I did not know. I would not have left again had I known I would never see her again. Forgive."

For hours he remained at the altar. His mind raced over the events of the last months: the sins he had committed in what he had done and failed to do. At last Albert felt the touch of a comforting hand on his shoulder as he wept in silence with his eyes closed. At first he thought Father Julien had come back to speak to him, but then he was distracted from his penance as he noticed the smallness of the hand. Shaking his head he rose unsteadily from the altar and turned to face a familiar old woman.

Madame Mannette had always been a close friend of Heloise. She spent much of her time helping Father Julien at the church, preparing breakfast for the children of the poor. She stood a full foot shorter than Albert. Gazing up at him with pity she said, "It is late, dear boy. You should go."

"How long have I been here?"

"It is nearly dawn," the old woman replied. "And there is someone in the main sanctuary who has been waiting to speak with you."

Albert crossed himself out of habit and left the side chapel, slowly retracing his steps to the nave of the church. Sitting in the flickering light of the votive candles at the feet of Mary was the figure of a woman dressed in black. At the sound of his footstep she turned. It was Angelique. She stood and turned to face him, her belly round with the child, her face radiant in the candlelight.

Albert drew his breath in sharply and suddenly he felt on fire, burning with a strange understanding that God had loved him all along. He could not speak or move until she called him to her.

With a look of surprise Angelique placed her hand on her stomach. "Your son is moving. Saying '*Bonjour*, Papa.' Would you like to meet him?"

As he rushed toward her, he no longer doubted

God. Enfolding her in his arms he held her close and rocked her, repeating her name again and again.

Behind the couple Father Julien cleared his throat. "She has been waiting for you. Praying you would come. Again you are sent from God."

"Will you marry us, Father? This morning?" Albert did not release his hold on her. "Angelique and our baby will bear my name as I will proudly bear the name of my heavenly Father. Will you help me set right my wrongs before I must leave again?"

"Like the knights of old, God has led you back home, Albert. And now we will celebrate the holy sacrament of your marriage."

Albert's head was aswirl: losing Angelique, finding her again, now on his way to Spain by way of the one clue to his identity. A few days were not enough time to take it all in; he would need a lifetime with Angelique to sort it out. His thoughts rattled around like musketballs in an empty gourd. He had reported in to the commandant of the navy forces at Brest and been told that his transport to Spain, the frigate *St. Denis*, would leave on the noon tide. Until then he was free to pursue his own investigations.

The black autumn clouds above the city of Brest were swollen with the threat of rain. Narrow, twisting alleyways led up from the quay. Brothels, dilapidated houses, and shops leaned over the center of the lane, nearly shutting out all daylight. The rank smells of sewage and too-ripe fish filled Albert's nostrils as he climbed the steps of Fishmonger's Lane toward the last-known residence of Francois D'Chiminee.

A haggard prostitute called out to him from an upper-story window. "Do not let the sailors find you here, Monsieur Hussar! They will get blood on your pretty blue tunic. Would you like to hide here with me awhile?"

"I am looking for Francois D'Chiminee."

"D'Chiminee? The smuggler? What does a handsome soldier like you want with the likes of him? Does he owe you money too?"

"An old friend of my grandmother's."

"*Oui?* Your grandmother? An old debt then. You'll have trouble getting anything out of that one." She wagged a grimy finger at him.

"You know him then." Albert was undeterred by her suggestive sneer.

"Know D'Chiminee? I know of him. I admit to nothing more. I only accept paying customers. The only true love he embraces these days is a jug of cheap wine. He will do anything for her, monsieur. You'll find him kissing her neck in the cellar of Dumas, barrelmaker at the top of the alley." She laughed and waved him on.

The workshop of Dumas, the cooper, was at the crest of a hill that looked down over the harbor. The doors of the workshop and warehouse were thrown wide to display a supply of newly made casks with which to provision Napoleon's navy. It was plain that the war had made the cooper prosperous. Six apprentices were hard at work shaping staves and assembling barrels. Dumas occupied a desk at the back of the workshop. With quill pen in hand, he pored over a ledger.

Albert entered the studio and received a cursory glance from one of the young workmen. "Papa," he called, "the army is here for their order."

Albert assumed he was the subject of the remark. "Pardon, monsieur. I am looking for one Monsieur Francois D'Chiminee."

With this comment all work halted. The old cooper stood up abruptly from his account book and hobbled forward to examine Albert suspiciously.

"Who are you?" he inquired, rubbing ink-stained fingers over his bald head.

Albert bowed curtly. "Albert Penfeld."

"Why have you come?"

Albert pulled the letter from his pocket. "The Prefecture of Police," he began, only to be cut short.

"Police. How much does Francois owe you then, monsieur?"

"Not a *sou*. I wish only to speak to him about personal business," Albert replied.

The cooper's shoulders sagged with relief. He hesitated a moment and then became aware that the sound of barrelmaking had stopped. He whirled on his assistants and loudly named off the list of military orders yet to be filled. Work resumed instantly, and the cooper turned his full attention back to Albert.

"To tell the truth I thought you were someone else—the army, you know. They want everything yesterday. I am relieved you are not here for casks," He almost smiled. "*Oui*. So, monsieur, le hussar Penfeld, you are a young gentlemen. What business can you have with my half brother?"

"He knew my grandmother. Some twenty years ago. Before she died she told me about his knowledge of some . . . well, some personal, family information."

"Since twenty years ago, monsieur, Francois has been slowly pickling his brains in bad wine." The cooper jerked his thumb toward a narrow flight of stairs leading to the cellar. "I give him a roof over his head and enough wine to keep him content. You'll find what there is of him down there. But I warn you, it is a pigsty, and he is the emperor of pigs."

The dimly lit cellar was crowded with barrels, iron hoops, staves, and stacks of lumber waiting to be shaped. Albert's heart was pounding as he made his way through the irregular passages to where a lantern hung on a hook in the stone wall.

He smelled D'Chiminee before he saw him sleeping on a bed of straw in the corner. The expected jug was tucked beneath his scrawny arm. His head lolled forward over the mouth of the container as though he had passed out before he swallowed. Filthy gray hair blended into a long, stained beard until the leathery face was nearly hidden by the tangle. His clothes were disheveled but not ragged. Apparently his half brother took care to see that D'Chiminee was dressed decently. A plate of uneaten bread and cheese was left on an upturned half-barrel that served as a table for the cubicle.

Albert's hopes fell as he observed the pitiful creature stretched out before him. Had twenty years of wine wiped out all memory of Albert's origins? "Monsieur D'Chiminee?" Albert's voice was loud to compete with the hammering upstairs. Still D'Chiminee did not move. Was he dead? Albert nudged him with the toe of his boot. The drunkard snorted and waved a hand in unconscious irritation.

Albert tried again. "Monsieur D'Chiminee! Francois D'Chiminee! Wake up, monsieur!"

The old man moaned a protest and held more tightly to his jug of wine. He opened one eye and glared angrily at Albert. "What do you want?"

"Monsieur, I have come a long way to meet you."

The head struggled upright; red-rimmed eyes stared at Albert. "What vision is this now? You are dressed too pretty to be from hell. They came to visit me last week. I saw them plain. Dressed in fire and calling me, they were. Bad wine, my brother said. But you, monsieur, all blue and gold buttons. An angel then?"

"No, Monsieur D'Chiminee. I am the baby you brought to Heloise Penfeld."

Silence. Stern contemplation. "Heloise? My old friend. How is she?"

"Regrettably, she is dead. My grandmother is dead."

"Dead? Heloise Penfeld? In heaven, that one. I have seen hell. And so there must be a heaven for Heloise." He took a long drink and sighed contentedly.

"*Oui.*" Albert stooped down beside him and placed a restraining hand on the jug. "She was a good woman. You found a baby from a shipwreck and brought me to her to care for and she did. Now I am grown, and I must. . . . Monsieur, do you remember what I am talking about?"

The aged smuggler said doubtfully, "It is too hard for me to remember yesterday, let alone years back."

"Think, I implore you. Heloise said you were the

greatest smuggler in all of Brittany. You found an infant. Where, monsieur? Think!"

Perhaps Albert's impassioned plea caused the fog of alcoholic vapors to part. D'Chiminee's eyes widened as if seeing something across a gap of twenty-some years. "Horrible," he said. "A dead man, drowned you see, floating on a cargo hatch. He was perhaps thirty, richly dressed. I thought . . . perhaps a watch, maybe even gold. I touched him and then a sound tore my heart in two!" D'Chiminee's face stretched with remembered terror.

"What?"

"A baby . . . tied beneath the man, but living—you!"

Albert acknowledged the truth. "But what of the man? Who was he?"

The smuggler slumped back against the wall. "No papers, nothing. But. . ."

"But what?" Albert demanded fiercely.

"His clothing. I think, English?"

Now it was Albert who rocked backward against the damp stones of the passage. "English," he repeated. "*Mon Dieu*, can it be?" Then, "The date," he demanded, grabbing the sagging D'Chiminee by his lapels. "What was the date?"

Of this fact D'Chiminee seemed more certain. "The great tempest. Truly the gale *a'outrance*. October, I think. Yes, October of 1780."

That was all. Nothing Albert could do or say would coax another word from the half-conscious man. To himself he murmured, "But it is something. How many ships were lost in October of 1780? I will search." He sat on a curbstone and pondered how he could make inquiries in England when there was a war on.

The bells of the Church of St. Louis were already chiming twelve before Albert broke out of his reverie. Twelve o'clock! He was supposed to be aboard the *St. Denis* at that very moment.

Dashing through the crowded streets, Albert arrived just in time to see the frigate dipping her colors in response to the salute fired by the Fort de la Pointe. He had missed it.

No, the commandant told him, there was no way to catch the frigate; she was too fast. Besides, he did not have ships available for careless young cavalrymen to have at their beck and call.

"But I must be aboard her," Albert pleaded. "It is most urgent."

The commandant pondered. "There is one possibility," he allowed. "She must put in at Paimpol for additional provisioning. But then, that is absurd—you could never reach. . ."

Albert was already racing toward the stables without waiting for the rest.

CHAPTER 13

Albert rode all night, following the route along the seacoast that led from Brest to the tiny harbor of Paimpol. Over and over he chastised himself for having missed the sailing of the *St. Denis.* Every time the leather pouch of his sabertache flapped against his leg, Albert was reminded of the official communiqué it contained. The package, sealed with both personal and imperial seals, was, to Albert's desperate imagination, hot to the touch.

Knowing that the pace he must adopt would be killing, Albert stabled Balthasar in Brest and took post horses for the journey. Changing mounts six times along the way, Albert had never ceased demanding a full canter for more than ten minutes at a time. He covered the one hundred-some miles to Paimpol in eleven hours, finally arriving at one in the morning.

Paimpol was a minuscule town and an even tinier harbor, built on the meager wealth of the cod fishery. As Albert galloped the rapidly tiring horse past the thirteenth-century Church of St. Anne he shuddered at the monument to local fishermen, lost at sea in Iceland's frigid seas: the bronze of a hooded female figure brooded on a stone plinth, cradling the body of an obviously drowned sailor. Albert shivered again. The sea had always terrified him, ever since childhood, but only now did he understand why.

The river outlet was a pleasant sight in the lantern light that shimmered on its windblown surface. Albert was exhausted and sore from the constant ride and could think of nothing he would like better than to collapse on the salty beach and sleep until morning. Instead, he drove his horse harder, covering the last mile quickly.

The sleepy port was already rising as fishermen prepared their trawlers for the day's catch, grumbling about the cold morning. Finding the dock where St. Denis's launch waited was easy, marked as promised by three lanterns hanging close together. Gratefully dismounting for the last time, Albert hobbled bowlegged to the edge of the wooden planks, and spotted a soldier napping in the rowboat.

Some distance out, the silhouette of a single frigate

rocked gently at anchor, its position noted by a solitary masthead light. It had to be the *St. Denis*. Albert imagined the bunk that would be prepared for him to rest and nearly drifted off with the thought. "*Bon soir*," he called, startling the sentry from his sleep. The soldier groggily looked away to the east, then started upright, demanding Albert identify himself.

"Gently," Albert suggested. "I am the courier, Albert Penfeld. Captain Bayonne was expecting me in Brest but..."

"You were late," the guard concluded.

"*Oui*, and I have ridden long and hard to rejoin you here," Albert said, grouchy at the unnecessary conversation. "Can we go aboard then?" he added wearily, hopping gingerly down to the lower gangway. "Let's be off." He climbed into the bow of the small launch as the oarsman loosed thin mooring line. The calming rhythm of the oars clapping gently on the hull and swirling water carried Albert to sleep, though the voyage lasted only a few minutes.

When at last the launch bumped into the hull of the *St. Denis*, Albert jumped from his rest, patting his sky-blue pelisse for the weighty package wrapped therein. Finding it still safe, he mounted the rope ladder over the siderail and onto the deck.

A lone figure loomed up out of the darkness.

"Captain Bayonne?"

"Watch Officer Tennant," the man corrected. "I'll go rouse the captain."

Albert leaned heavily against the mainmast and nearly fell asleep again before the captain emerged from below deck, tucking a nightshirt over his large belly and into his unbuttoned trousers. "Captain Bayonne," he said, touching a hand lazily to his bald head, returning Albert's salute.

"When do we sail?" Albert demanded.

"Now you are in a rush?" said the portly officer, yawning. "Not before the morning tide."

There was nothing further to be done. His mind too tired for anything other than the notion of a few hour's undisturbed rest, Albert asked, "Where can I sleep?"

Captain Bayonne raised a stubby finger and turned toward the gangway. "Follow me." Albert was introduced to a three-bunk room near the captain's cabin. Two of the bunks were occupied by junior officers who did not even awaken at the trespasser's arrival. Albert fell onto the plank bed, drifting at once to sleep.

No more than an hour later by Albert's estimation, he was awakened by a lurch in the ship's otherwise steady rocking. There was the clatter of running feet, the strident ringing of a bell, and then two cannonblasts went off in close succession.

Albert's two slumbering companions had grabbed trousers and swords and dashed out of the cabin before Albert could even collect his thoughts to ask what was happening. The answer came clearly in ringing tones repeated through the chain of command: "Prepare to repel boarders!"

Breathing hard, Albert listened to the building commotion. More cannonfire erupted and the rattle of musketry was added to the din. French voices shouted, accompanying heavy footsteps running up the gangway. Albert yanked on his uniform and boots, buckled on his sword belt, started up the gangway, then turned back to retrieve the sabertache and hang it around his neck.

More shots sounded as Albert dashed along the companionway, coming face-to-face with Captain Bayonne. The officer was pale, wringing his shaking hands.

"What is it?" Albert hissed.

"English! They've boarded the ship!"

Albert thought quickly about the package under his care. "Have you weapons in your cabin?"

"Yes," Bayonne said, "but the key. . ."

"Where?" Albert shook him by the shoulders.

Bayonne reached into the neck of his nightshirt and removed a necklace with a brass key hanging from it. Albert snatched the brass rod from the captain's clammy hand and charged into the captain's cabin. An iron-barred locker located near the bed opposite the door contained three musketoons and five pistols. Albert quickly opened it, seizing four pistols. Running back to the hallway, he handed two to Bayonne who just looked at them in his hands as if they were unrecognizable.

Albert gritted his teeth and charged up the gangway. Instantly he saw how many crew had already been killed, their bodies sprawled awkwardly around the deck, some still gripping their weapons. Near the port bow, some of the French crew fought off more invaders, but musketfire from the quarterdeck behind him struck them in the back, dropping them one by one to the wood. Albert spun around and backed away from the hatch with pistols raised.

A British soldier sprang forward with a musket leveled at Albert's head, but a look of quandary came over him, and he did not fire. Not stopping to wonder at the miraculous deliverance of what would have been certain death, Albert seized the moment and bounded for the starboard side, throwing himself overboard and swimming for the quay.

As Albert swam, he heard the dying roar of the battle that raged on the ship and wondered if any of the Frenchmen aboard were still alive. He waded the last few feet to dry land, then collapsed on the shore. Why had the British soldier not fired, he wondered as a fitful sleep overtook him. Shivering through the remaining hours of darkness, he was glad when it was morning. The sun warmed him on the sand and seemed to energize him.

"I still have a mission," he said to himself as he rose from the gritty earth. Looking back into the harbor, he realized again the consequences of the fact that the ship was gone.

In the water he had lost his bearings and swum south by mistake, carried by the current, coming to land around a rocky point by the village of Treville. It would be at least a half day's walk to any civilization. Trudging miserably in heavy, soggy clothing, he moved southward, hoping to reach Treville by noonday.

It was one o'clock by the time he reached the village. Along the way he had removed all but his trousers to keep from overheating. As he passed the meager huts on the outskirts, the fisherfolk gawked at him, wondering, he imagined, if he were a deserter. When at last he came to a residence with a swaybacked horse pegged in a field of salt grass, he could find no one home.

Albert would not have taken the animal without explaining and he would have left some money for it, but his cash had been lost during his rigorous swim to shore. Everything, in fact, except for the orders still tucked inside the sabertache. He wondered if they would even be legible after being soaked for so long.

He shook the thought from his mind. "I must deliver the message, no matter what condition the orders, or I, for that matter, am in." With those last words, he mounted the horse bareback, having found no saddle in the owner's tackroom. The big bay was quickly bridled with a harness so old it must have arrived in Gaul with the legions of Julius Caesar. It chewed torpidly on the bit as Albert jumped on its back. Albert dreaded another long ride, especially with no padding between his backside and the horse's, but maneuvered the horse confidently away from the house and on southward.

Despite constant kicking to the flanks, Albert could not inspire the beast to move any faster than a dogged trot, and the jolts pained him constantly. Returning to Paimpol was no use; there were no other fast ships in harbor anyway. Figuring the mileage to the next port of some size and the pace of the beast, Albert wondered if the war would be over by the time he delivered his orders.

Nearly three hours later, Albert reached Quimper. There he hoped that he could obtain a fresh horse and move faster.

It was from a militia cavalry unit that he acquired another rested, well-fed, trained, and most important to

Albert, saddled, remount. The captain of the unit had encouraged him to rest and let another of his men carry the orders until Albert explained the direct nature under which they had come from Napoleon.

Bowing to the urgency of the need, the captain instead sent two other soldiers along with Albert as protection. He also suggested that they make for Lorient, another coastal town to the south, and try to board another ship there. He had heard the navy had a large gunship in port there. The ride to Lorient would take another nine hours.

Four hours later, Albert's horse stopped. As luck would have it, this occurred no more than fifteen minutes after his traveling companions reached the end of their road and, bidding him "*Bon chance!*" had departed.

The horse refused to move farther, and when he spurred it, began a slow kneel toward the ground.

Albert yelled at himself, "You've killed it!" Quickly he dismounted, and the beast rose at once and trotted away from him. When he went after it, it bolted off the dirt road and into the woods.

He clutched his head in both hands. "Oh, God," he said. Exhausted and frustrated, he sat down in the road and wept. "Will I never make it?"

It was dark again, and Albert could not contemplate

moving another inch. Overcome, he fell asleep there in the middle of a dirt track midway between lost and nowhere.

As the sun rose on the third day of his troubled journey, he lay awake but unmoving in the road.

"I can't go on," he said, the breath from his words scattering dust under his face. With one eye open, he watched an ant scurry toward his outstretched left hand. It moved up his forefinger to the knuckle, paused, and twitched. It seemed to look right at Albert with its shiny black eyes, then it bit him.

Albert jumped up, slapping the back of his hand with the other. The ant flew to the ground, and Albert raised a foot to crush it. Poised for the kill, he heard a thundering noise drawing near and paused. It soon became distinguishable as the pounding of hooves and the groaning of a heavily loaded wagon.

The ant scurried away, and Albert scratched the bite as he moved from the road. As the wagon rounded a bend, the driver reined the team to a stop near Albert. Another wagon drew up behind, then another. The driver was a sea soldier wearing the dark-blue, short-waisted jacket and red sash that identified his service. On his head was a flat-crowned leather hat with the front brim turned up. Albert called to him in an unsure voice, *"Bonjour."*

"Hello," came the reply. "Unless you have been scavenging in the leftovers of a cavalry regiment, my friend, you are in a bad way. What are you doing out here alone?"

Feeling as if his oft-repeated explanation must be sounding as tired as he himself, Albert nevertheless retold it and all the events of the past two days.

"Amazing!" the soldier said. "We are delivering supplies to the sloop-of-war *Montpellier* in Lorient. Powder and shot destined for the fastest ship in the fleet! Come, we will be there in only a few hours. What is more, we are off to rejoin the fleet. Should they sail to the Antipodes," he said, snapping his fingers, "we will follow and overtake them."

Albert climbed aboard the wagon, taking a seat next to the driver, who introduced himself as Master Sergeant Coccinelle.

"Have no fear," Sergeant Coccinelle reassured Albert. "The *Montpellier* cannot sail without us and our supplies. *Eh bien*, she cannot sail without you either. Once aboard, she does not swim; she flies! We will assist you in your mission to locate the good admiral. Why, *diable!* You will make better time now than if you had been on that old slow-coach of a frigate anyway!"

Despite the torments of the past days, it was impossible to be melancholy around the irrepressible Sergeant

Coccinelle. Best of all, his predictions came true: Albert was welcomed aboard *Montpellier*, which delayed only long enough to get her provisions aboard before weighing anchor and setting course southwest. Before the port of Lorient had even dropped from sight astern, the *Montpellier* was making ten knots, and Albert was feeling more reassured than at any moment since leaving Paris.

William lay restless in his hammock. He urged himself to sleep, turned over, and thought longingly of Dora. Only two weeks at sea, and yet it seemed impossible to fall asleep without thinking of her, as much as he resisted the idea. *Maybe thinking of her is the only way to stop thinking of her,* he reasoned. *Maybe writing her and letting her know how I feel is the only way for me to get over what I'm feeling, or at least to get around it for the time at hand.*

He rolled from his hammock to his bare feet, climbing around a cannon to open his sea bag beneath the fitful glow of the passage lantern. The gunport was cracked open slightly to admit some air. All around him his messmates were snoring. The room, crammed full of men in hammocks, seemed stuffed with canvas-wrapped sausages. Perching on a twenty-four-pound cannonball, he sat down on the shot garland and leaned back against the bulkhead with a sheet of notepaper to begin writing.

"Dear Dora," William began. He must have crumpled a dozen sheets before finding the right words to come after the greeting. "I miss you. . . . No, too vulnerable. I've thought about you quite frequently. . . . Too desperate. I agree with what you said that night. . . . Oh bother!" He wadded another page into a ball and threw it as hard as he could out the hatch of the gunport. It streamed out, trailing behind in the wind, before disappearing somewhere in the foamy wake.

He heard a voice in his head. *William, don't try to hide what you have to say.*

William considered the voice, then quietly argued with it. "But now is not the time to fall in love. Now is the time to look ahead, not behind."

Listen to your heart, William, the whisper commanded softly. *Go where it tells you to go.*

"No. Not yet. I couldn't take it if her feelings have changed. For now I must remain as I am." He peeked out over the vast miles of open ocean. "But at the same time, I must know how she is. I know. I shall write a letter to Father Donspy and tell him of the action I have recently seen."

William began his letter,

Dear Father Donspy,
I am writing in gratitude for the kindly world which

you shared with me, the family and the new under-standing of a life worth living. Thank you. I hope the family is well. Give my affectionate regards to Mrs. Donspy and to Dora. Many times during the day my mind returns to the long meadow at the bottom of the hill where we drilled. I think of the Branson Fen Militia, and I can't help but wonder how they are doing. I have recently seen some fighting. It is a story you may find interesting, and I'm sure will want to share with the rest.

Four days ago, while shadowing a portion of the French fleet, we were running down the coast of Brittany. It was almost nightfall when we came up in the lee of a headland. The lookout called down that he had seen the masts of a ship moored up in a harbor named Paimpol only a few miles up the coast. Confident we were unremarked, Captain O'Brian called all the marines to ready a boarding party for a boat action. . . .

That night the British frigate *Pegasus* had moored up out of sight of the other French ship, the *St. Denis*. Loaded with muskets, powder cages and shot, boarding axes and cutlasses, every marine and forty-two more navy ratings put on dark clothing and blackened their faces with burnt cork. The davits were lowered, and six longboats set quietly down in the water.

Careful not to make even a single splash, the men began softly rowing, the oarlocks muffled in rags. A moonless night had fallen, so there was hardly any light in the sky. Six miles they rowed before rounding the point, under the silent guns of a shore battery, before spotting the ship fast asleep in the harbor. William mentally readied himself for battle. His blood ran cold, and he had the same breathless, jittery feeling he had experienced before every physical confrontation. Above all, he promised himself that he would return alive. He wondered briefly about those who would not. Just the thought made him grip his musket more tightly.

A gun boomed from the deck of the warship. So the surprise had been lost after all! A shot sailed over their heads, whistling close by. William turned his head to see where it collided with the water. A geyser shot thirty feet in the air.

The six longboats separated and spread out. All the men abandoned caution and strained their hardest now. It was essential to close the gap in haste, before they were blown out of the water.

The deck of their goal livened with bodies rushing to every station. Cannonfire grew rapidly more regular.

Grapeshot pelted the waves away around the little boats, though none had yet been hit.

William flipped up the sight on his musket. He scanned the decks of the ship in search of a target. Then he saw a French sailor hanging in the rigging, directing the fire of a deck gun. William squeezed the trigger. A second later he saw the man flinch and spasm backward out the lines and toward the deck. But by then William was already reloading and seeking another target.

The longboats were nearing contact. One had been totally shattered by that first shot, but the others were virtually unscathed. At such a close distance they were safe from cannonfire as the guns could not be depressed enough to hit them. However, their dangers came from another form.

The French sailors and marines leaned out over the sides with muskets and rifles. The snap and roar of flint-locks twined with the screams of men hit in the boats. Two longboats kept apart, some thirty yards off, to continue firing against the deck. Meanwhile, William's boat swept toward the anchor and the bowsprit. It and two others met at the bow of the ship, intending to board by throwing grappling hooks over the cats and the main-chains.

William slung his rifle over his shoulder and began climbing up. Two steps up a man leaned out of a gunport a few feet away and took aim. William froze, and then just before he was shot, someone still in the longboat fired, striking the Frenchman in the face. William climbed on.

When William got to the top, there was no time to reload his musket. He swarmed over the netting, drew his cutlass, and charged the first Frenchman he spotted. The match was quickly over. William, using the cutlass more like a club than a sword, smashed his opponent aside with a heavy blow.

William realized that the only way to make it through alive was to move fast enough that no one had time to come up behind him. The constant chill of fear drove him on, and he let out a mad shriek, charging into another man and bowling him over. William lifted the struggling Frenchman and tossed him over the side.

At first, progress to gain more deck was slow. When all had boarded, the Royal Marines charged from the bow sternward, cutting down everything in their path.

William led the charge. At one point he was completely surrounded by French soldiers. He spun around in a circle, slashing at three men to keep them back. Then he was joined by four of his comrades, and the French gave ground.

Abruptly one of his messmates groaned and toppled over, his shoulder shattered by a musketball fired from above. William spotted the sniper in the maintop reloading.

Jamming his sword into the deck in front of him, William pulled his musket around. From his cartridge box he removed a paper cartridge, tearing it open with his teeth and taking the lead ball in his mouth. He filled the pan, dumped the rest of the powder into the muzzle, spat the ball into his palm, and pressed it in after the powder.

William fumbled to free the ramrod from the barrel. It was jammed, bent somehow in the fighting. He raised his eyes and saw that the Frenchman was drawing down again. Jamming the ramrod home, William swung the musket to his shoulder without further hesitation.

The exploding charge blasted ramrod and all straight at the sniper, who fired at that same instant.

Two clouds of smoke marked where the bullets came from and where they were going. The metal rod flew as straight as an arrow, piercing the chest of the Frenchman. He plunged out of the rigging. William was only grazed on the neck.

Yanking his cutlass free from the plank, William took up the fight once again. To his left, a redcoat fell and toward the stern, another. He wondered if they were winning or losing. Blood from his neck wound soaked his collar and chest. The cold air made the wound sting, but William did not notice. He kept on fighting at full force until finally the party from the bow was joined by that from the stern, led by Thomas.

The French captain lay dead; the French lieutenant struck the colors, giving up the fight. With ninety-three Frenchmen killed or wounded to only eleven killed from the *Pegasus*, it was a marvelous victory for the English.

The marines rousted out the now-weaponless Frenchmen. As they rounded up the prisoners, one of William's messmates, a Newcastle man named Darlington, called to him breathlessly, "William! William!"

William, holding a bandage over his wound, turned around to see what he was about.

"William, I'm so sorry."

William was confused by his apology. "Sorry for what?"

Darlington looked at him as if surely he must know. "For almost shooting you."

"Almost shooting me?"

"Yes. I saw a man in a French cavalry rig, and when I raised my musket to fire, it was you! Thank God you looked me right in the face, and when I hesitated, you dived over the side."

William laughed. "The powder smoke has done your head a mischief."

"I'm positive of what I saw. Come now! Where is your dangerous disguise?"

William was baffled. "It was not me, I can promise you. See for yourself."

Darlington looked him up and down, feeling his clothes. "They're not wet." Now he too was confused. "But I saw you dive over the side. . . ."

"Strange are the effects of war," William replied, walking away. "Let's get ready to get under way, before the French fort decides it would be worth slaughtering their own men to keep this ship out of English hands."

When William concluded his account in the letter to Father Donspy, William failed to mention that he was assigned to the prize crew aboard the *St. Denis*.

CHAPTER 14

The night was brilliantly lit by the moon. A light breeze from nor-norwest blew just enough to stir the calm waters, causing the tips of each swell to sparkle like a million tiny diamonds stretching as far as the eye could see. William, in his newly promoted rank of second lieutenant of marines, stood on the quarterdeck of the captured *St. Denis*, somewhere near the narrowest part of the English Channel. Breathing deeply, he took in all the serenity the night and the ocean could offer. William was enjoying sea life, though wishing Thomas could share his success with him. Thomas had his own duties, two hours behind on the *Pegasus*.

The lookout called down from the maintop to the sailing master. "Ahoy, below. Sails dead ahead."

Lieutenant Meecham, as acting captain of the captured vessel, ordered the *St. Denis* to fall off a point, so as to give him a clearer view ahead. The height of the masts on the approaching vessel and the acres of canvas she carried showed her to be a much larger vessel than the *St. Denis*. To launch the rockets of the recognition signal would give away their position to a potential enemy, so Lieutenant Meecham elected to run.

The course was soon reversed, and the frigate running before the wind. That they had been spotted was soon evident as the lookout shouted that the pursuer had also altered course. A spiteful flight of chainshot from the shore battery at Paimpol had left the *St. Denis* with damaged main and mizzen rigging and without her customary turn of speed.

Meecham, peering through the night scope, studied the newcomer and calmly announced, "She's French, right enough. I make her out to be a heavy frigate. Forty guns, I should think."

William knew that, damaged as they were, the *St. Denis* could not hope to escape. The latter information meant she was outgunned as well.

By the hooded binnacle light the sailing master consulted a list of enemy vessels known to be in those waters. "She could be the *Le Havre*, sir," he suggested.

"Yes," Meecham murmured thoughtfully. "She carries twenty-eight eighteen pounders on her gun deck." Left unspoken was the comparison with the paltry eight pounders with which the main battery of the *St. Denis* was equipped.

William hurried to his place on the main deck to prepare for battle. A double rank of marines lined each rail. As the hammocks came up from below, William and the others stowed them in the netting forming the bulwarks.

A blue rocket burst above the pursuing ship. This signal was followed by a group of three red lanterns being displayed. "French recognition signal, sir," Midshipman Moore reported.

Meecham grimaced. "Fire a gun to windward and hoist red-white-red," he ordered. "We'll see if last month's signal is still good."

The response from the French ship was not long in coming. There was a jet of flame from her foredeck, a whistle through the rigging in the *St. Denis*'s foretop and a splash on the far side. "Bless me," Lieutenant Meecham observed. "It is the *Le Havre* for certain. She mounts eight-pounder long guns as bow chasers."

The order to heave-to and await the *Le Havre*'s approach went down through the ranks. There was some grumbling at this seeming lack of fighting spirit, but William quelled it by noting, "Button it up, lads, and look sharp. Lieutenant Meecham has something up his sleeve."

Not much time passed before the French first lieutenant, Beaulieu by name, was aboard the *St. Denis* and accepting Meecham's sword in token of surrender. "You were right to recognize the inevitable, Captain," Beaulieu remarked as the officers were herded aft into the captain's cabin and the men driven below decks forward. "And Admiral the Marquis Serceyl will be gracious since we have recaptured a French ship."

It was at the same moment as the bolt clicked, locking up the British officers, that William thought of the *Pegasus* sailing down to meet them, by now only an hour or so behind. Meecham held up his hand for silence, then made signals confirming to the officers exactly what William had guessed.

On the deck of the *St. Denis*, repairs were being made to the damaged rigging when Lieutenant Beaulieu was alerted to a vessel running south by east toward them. By listening at the captain's skylight, the prisoners could overhear the discussion taking place on the quarterdeck just above their heads. Meecham understood French, as did William.

"The approaching vessel has no lights," William heard a midshipman report, "and they sail toward us as if we are not here."

Lieutenant Beaulieu apparently studied the newcomer awhile through his glass because there was a pause before he observed, "It must be a merchantman, to run down so unaware. Probably the lookout is asleep. Nevertheless, we will be cautious. Signal the *Le Havre* that another vessel is in sight, then fire a shot across her bow."

"*Oui*, Lieutenant."

The command was given, and a moment later, one of the *St. Denis*'s own six-pound cannonballs was fired at the new arrival, splashing immediately under her bow and ricocheting up to strike her on the starboard side. Still the ship did not respond but sailed submissively into French hands.

"It looks to be an English frigate," Beaulieu commented. "But why are there no lights?" He watched as the vessel moved closer yet. Examining the deck through his glass, it appeared there was no movement. Seeing no colors, he was befuddled until the ship was extremely close.

Suddenly from the foremast the flag of Great Britain floated free, and the *Pegasus* sprang into action. Men jumped from under cannon and cover, firing every gun at once. The *St. Denis* shook with a thunderous crash when the broadside ripped through the unready decks.

"They're here!" William exclaimed. "The *Pegasus* has caught them napping."

Then the French manning the guns of the *St. Denis* fired in earnest to join the battle.

Lieutenant Meecham and William took turns spying through the windows of the captain's gallery as the battle raged on. Several times a shot from the *Pegasus* battered the walls of the cabin in which the captives were held. It made William think twice about his protected state, off-deck and hidden from the action. It made him more afraid than reassured, not knowing if at any moment the next shot might crash through the wall right where he was sitting. After several more near misses, Meecham ordered the officers to lie down on the floor. Moments after this movement, a shot burst through the wall and smashed the chest on which William had been standing to smithereens.

Captain O'Brian, on the *Pegasus*, carried the battle to recapture the *St. Denis* by engaging her on the side opposite to the *Le Havre*. The French aboard the larger vessel did not want to risk shelling their own frigate, so for a time the contest was between vessels of roughly equal strength.

It could not last, though. After one pass and another broadside, the *Pegasus* found herself between the guns of the two French vessels. Chainshot smashed her rigging, and the carronades of the *Le Havre*, useless at long range but powerfully deadly close-up, smashed the British masts into stumps.

William saw the mainmast of the *Pegasus*, looking like a headless one-armed figure holding a fluttering white cape by the yards that remained. Her deck was a twisted mass of canvas and rigging, with men trapped underneath.

It was then that Captain O'Brian ordered a change of tactics, and with the last steerageway the *Pegasus* possessed, he aimed her amidships of the *Le Havre*. The *Pegasus* endured withering fire before the two ships collided, but when they had collided and the *Pegasus* was lashed firmly to the side of the larger ship, the balance of firepower shifted.

The *Le Havre*'s massive armament was no use when it towered a full deck higher than the clinging *Pegasus*. While the guns of the British frigate were elevated to fire up through the hull of the *Le Havre*, the French could not depress their cannons enough to damage the *Pegasus*.

William saw the remaining Royal Marines swarm out of the damaged *Pegasus* and up the side of the French ship. He thought he recognized Thomas with them, but in the darkness lit by muzzle flashes and burning timbers, he could not be certain.

"Now, lads," Lieutenant Meecham ordered, "now's our

time. The French over our heads will be all akimbo, not knowing what to do. We can retake the *St. Denis* now."

And so it proved. The door burst out to the impact of William's shoulder. The sentries outside the captain's cabin were overpowered after firing two shots that went unheard amid the battle. Armed with cutlasses from the *St. Denis*'s armory, soon Meecham and his men swept the quarterdeck. William pinned Lieutenant Beaulieu against the mizzenmast and demanded his surrender.

That was when it happened. Without warning the amidships section of the *Pegasus* exploded, erupting into the night sky and spilling men, timbers, and cannons into the sea. The first explosion set off a chain reaction, and the ship ripped in short bursts, all the way to the bow. Then a final explosion erupted, scattering shards of wood and bodies everywhere. Shrapnel even pelted the *St. Denis*, causing William to flinch away, but horrific fascination drove him back.

When he looked again, the *Pegasus* had completely disappeared from sight. The only sign that it had sunk was the bubbling pit in the ocean.

By the fortunes of war, the explosion alongside the *Le Havre* annihilated the British frigate, but actually killed more of the French belowdecks working the guns. The thunderclap that destroyed the *Pegasus* seemed to paralyze the French, while it made the British fight harder—this and the fact that flying debris had killed both the French admiral and the *Le Havre's* captain turned the tide of the battle. Within moments of the massive explosion, both the *Le Havre* and the *St. Denis* were in English hands.

Both captured French ships were repaired. The *Le Havre*, as the more badly damaged of the two, was sent back to England with the prisoners and the *Pegasus's* mail chest, found floating amid the debris. To this grim set of postmortem messages was appended a list of all who had been aboard the *Pegasus* but who had survived the fight and the cataclysmic detonation. The list did not include William's name, since he was already aboard the *St. Denis*. This distinction was not explained in the dispatch, however.

Miraculously, Thomas and Captain O'Brian survived. Both men joined William aboard the *St. Denis*. They then parted from the *Le Havre* and headed off to join the English fleet at the blockade of Cadíz.

"Heroic Action & Tragic Loss" announced the broadsheet tacked to the public notice board in the town square at Branson Fen. "The HMS *Pegasus*, after capturing the French frigate the *St. Denis*, was hotly engaged with another French ship, the *Le Havre*, when she tragically blew up."

"Oh, Father!" Dora pleaded. "Read it to me! I am too afraid to read it for myself."

"Miraculously," the handbill continued, "many of the crew of the *Pegasus* were spared as they were attacking their opponent on her own decks. The result of the action is that our gallant seamen have captured two French warships, at the regrettable cost of the *Pegasus* and some valiant men."

"Hurry, Father!" Dora urged. "Get to the casualty list."

"Be brave, Daughter," Father Donspy insisted. "Yes, here it is, on a separate sheet."

"Owing to the unusual circumstance of the disaster," the notice read, "we list here the names of those daring men known to have survived the conflagration. All others are missing and presumed lost."

William's name was not on the list.

The cannon on the parade ground fired three muffled charges at sunset, and the militia wore black armbands atop their green uniforms.

Dora Donspy sat alone in her darkened room, crying.

Albert hastened to Admiral Villeneuve's flagship, the *Bucentaure*, as soon as he arrived. His journey down the coast aboard the *Montpellier* had been as fast as promised, taking only four days to arrive in Cadíz. This, her captain claimed, was a record, all the more remarkable since she had been hugging the coast the last three hundred miles to avoid an enormous concentration of British warships.

Albert had been seasick for much of the passage. His uniform was cleaned and his buttons polished, but his face still bore a hint of green when he was ushered into the admiral's quarters in the stern gallery of the eighty-gun ship-of-the-line. The two men were alone.

"Good heavens," Admiral Villeneuve exclaimed, looking at the sadly wrinkled, weathered document. "What on earth have you done to this dispatch?" He broke the wax seal and removed the contents.

As he unfolded the papers within, Albert tried to look over the top of the document to see if the words were legible after being submersed that first evening.

Admiral Villeneuve noticed his interest and held the paper higher, scowling at him for trying to read it. Albert tried to explain why he was interested, but Villeneuve took no notice. Instead he read on, and Albert noticed a queer change of the admiral's skin. It turned a bright red and it appeared to Albert that his head might pop if the pressure were not relieved. "Do you know what is contained in this document?" the admiral demanded.

Albert was forced to acknowledge that, yes, he was aware of the subject.

"What can the emperor be thinking of?" Villeneuve fumed. "Replacing me with that old man Rossily? Did I not elude the British all the way to the Indies and back? Did I not preserve them intact . . . thirty-three of the most powerful weapons of war in the world? I tell you I . . ." The torrent of words broke off abruptly as he realized he was speaking his mind too freely in front of a stranger.

Admiral Villeneuve dropped the paper to his side, mirroring the action his jaw had just taken, then he called his flagship captain to join him in consultation. "He's asked me to step down." The admiral's voice was a whisper.

The *Bucentaure*'s captain fired a battery of questions at the weary-faced admiral. "What? Who? Step down . . . from what?"

"Napoleon," Admiral Villeneuve said, turning away to face his cabin wall. "The emperor has relieved me of my command for not being more aggressive toward the British. Does he have a crystal ball into which he can gaze?" Villeneuve said bitterly. "Can he predict the moments when safe passage is assured?"

Though Albert had no personal interest in Admiral Villeneuve's sad news, he knew better than to interrupt the unlucky man before him.

"He can't do this!" Villeneuve exclaimed, spinning from the wall and wiping a stream of tears from under his right eye. "I have served him well and faithfully for too long, and I'll be . . ." Admiral Villeneuve caught himself again, realizing Albert was still in the room. "Young man, thank you. Your duties have been completed. My steward, Brillac, will show you to a room where you may rest until dinner this evening."

Saluting, Albert spun smartly on his heel, then paused. "Your pardon, monsieur," he said. "Because of the water damage to the message, I feel it is my duty to be certain that all parts are understood. The second portion of the communiqué is that the emperor expressly forbids the fleet to sail until. . ." Albert lowered his tone and dropped his eyes. "Until Admiral Rossily has determined it is safe to proceed to the Mediterranean. On no account is an engagement with the British to be risked at this time. The emperor desires that the fleet be kept intact for next season's invasion."

Villeneuve impatiently waved away Albert's cautioning words. "Yes, yes," he said testily. "You need not tell me my duty."

Albert offered a stiff bow, which was not returned, and then followed the steward to his cabin. He did not notice a private signal that passed between Villeneuve and Brillac.

As the door closed behind him, Albert thought he heard a key turn in the lock. *That's strange*, he thought. When he tried the door, it was in fact bolted tight. He knocked and called, but no one replied.

Some time later he heard a tramp of footsteps in the companionway. When the door was opened, Albert found himself confronting a file of armed sailors. He was told he must make no noise, nor offer any resistance, and he would be left unbound.

"Unbound?" Albert exploded. "What is this about?"

"Fleet security," he was told. Admiral Villeneuve was concerned about British spies in Cadíz. For his own protection and the good of the fleet, Albert was being taken into custody.

Albert demanded to see the admiral at once and was told that Villeneuve was in a high-level conference and could not be disturbed. "But do not be alarmed," the bosun's mate assured Albert. "The admiral says to tell you that all will be explained tomorrow."

Once fed, even though locked in again, sleep was as immediate as it was inevitable. Albert had never fully rested while the orders were in his charge. Always he had been awakened by a dream of drowning, watching the wax-sealed docket float away from his grasp. Now that it had been delivered properly, he slept deeply.

CHAPTER 15

—————◆◆—————

Admiral Nelson had ordered that the blockading British men-of-war stay over the horizon, out of sight of the French and Spanish ships at Cadíz. His intent with this strategy was to gull the combined fleet into making a run for the straits of Gibraltar.

His stratagem succeeded. On the twentieth of October, 1805, the frigate *Euryalus* detected ships making sail and exiting the harbor. This message was relayed through signals to Nelson aboard his flagship, the HMS *Victory. Euryalus* and the other British frigates such as the captured French ship the *St. Denis,* were to act as watchdogs and messenger ships.

William was in the launch with Captain O'Brian when O'Brian was rowed to consult with the other captains aboard the *Victory.* William heard the repeated gossip of Nelson's words: "I will sail right at them. I want to bring on a pell-mell battle."

To his regret, William did not expect to take part in the upcoming engagement. Undergunned in comparison to ships-of-the-line, frigates were not intended to participate in the fleet action.

Then just as William was reembarking on the cutter to rejoin the *St. Denis*, Captain Adair of the *Victory*'s marine contingent stopped him. "The *Victory* is undermanned with marines," he said. "Lord Nelson has authorized the transfer of you and twenty of your men to our ranks."

So it was that when the sun rose on the morning of October twenty-first, William found himself aboard the flagship of the British fleet just as the sails of thirty-three enemy ships floated up out of the mist, the press of their masts looking like a linen-draped forest run away to sea.

On duty in the admiral's chart room, William was privy to all that passed between Captain Hardy and the other officers aboard the *Victory*. "Lord Nelson's ploy was a brilliant maneuver," Hardy remarked, pointing at a map. "They are hemmed by Cape Trafalgar and now cut off from Cadíz Harbor. They have no choice but to fight."

"Gentlemen," Fleet Surgeon William Beatty addressed them. "There is a concern of greater urgency,

I believe, than the confident speculation of our glorious victory."

All heads turned toward the older plump gentleman, who had a slightly balding head and bushy sidewhiskers. He spoke with a composed authority. "The concern of which I speak regards the chosen dress of his lordship." William observed a unanimous and solemn *yea* among the men. "For Lord Nelson to be so brash as to insist on wearing his dress uniform and all of his medals in battle, he will surely end up dead or seriously wounded."

Mr. Scott, the admiral's secretary aboard the HMS *Victory,* interrupted. "Dr. Beatty, such a request would have no good effect; and moreover his lordship will be highly displeased with any who should take the liberty of recommending such a change in his dress. So take care, Doctor, what you are about. I would not be the man to mention such a matter to him."

The matter was then dropped. Lord Nelson was making the rounds of the ship's hands, so as to instill confidence in them. It was but a few moments later that he arrived to set the final tactics into motion.

Such a little man, William thought, *to wield so much authority and inspire so much concern.* Nelson, who was missing one arm and one eye and was scarcely five inches more than five feet tall, rounded the table and all fell silent. His uniform coat was resplendent with no

fewer than four large gold and jewel-encrusted medal-
lions. He immediately spotted William as the newcomer
to the group.

"You must be Lieutenant William Sutton," Nelson
said as he introduced himself. "It is reported that you
fight bravely, particularly as you had to capture the *St.
Denis* not once but twice. You will be called upon again
today."

"Thank you, milord," William responded as Nelson
smiled with satisfaction at the anticipated battle.

"The enemy is ready, and the time is close at hand.
They number thirty-three to our twenty-seven. It is
clear they cannot avoid a general engagement this time.
To this I am exceedingly willing, for the entire fate of
England and the world may rest upon this day."

Despite the fact that the French and Spanish ships
were in full view already, the light winds made it impossible for the battle to begin in less than three hours.
Plenty of time to prepare and perhaps too much time to
think. All the mess furniture from the officer's quarters
was stowed away. Hammocks were pulled down from
the beams of the gun decks, rolled tightly, and stacked
around the perimeter of the decks as shielding. One of
the hammocks William rolled had huge holes in it. He
looked closely at the frayed rope. As he cinched up, he
could see that all the holes lined up. It was evident that

this bit of netting had tried to stop a cannonball, but by the look of things, had not succeeded.

William was not preoccupied with thoughts of the coming battle or of the danger to himself. He carried on with his duties, mechanically readying himself and his men.

What did come unexpectedly to his mind were thoughts of his long-lost twin brother. *How strange*, William mused, *that if Charles had lived, he would have come to this same age on this momentous day, the same as me. I wonder if he would be here, facing this same battle.*

In some ways he had lived his brother's life, having been granted the twenty-some years that his brother had been denied. Briefly he wondered if he might be joining his brother by the close of the day's events, but he hurriedly put that notion out of his mind.

When the sound of six bells of the forenoon watch, eleven o'clock, came to William's attention, he looked up. His notice, as well as that of the twenty thousand other men on the twenty-six British ships, was drawn to the signal flags that were run up the *Victory*'s rigging. He read them aloud. "England . . . Expects . . . That . . . Every . . . Man . . . Will . . . Do . . . His . . . Duty." The sight caused William to drop a bucket of sand to the deck. Watching wordlessly, he shivered with pride. The next few hours just *might* decide the fate of the world.

Some hours later Albert awoke, groggy and headachy. He felt seasick again and wondered at his weak constitution to become ill while riding at anchor in port. His door was unlocked, though no one had bothered to explain anything about why it had been locked in the first place.

Stumbling out of his cabin, Albert balanced against a slight rocking as he climbed the stairs to the quarter-deck.

The wind blew cold through his hair, and the salt mist coated his neck. When he heard the sound of rushing water, he knew they had put to sea. The deck was busy with sailors heaving at lines and officers shouting orders as they apparently prepared for a battle.

Albert cinched up his collar against the cold. There stood Admiral Villeneuve, hands clasped behind him in conscious or unconscious imitation of the emperor, as the fleet put to sea. "*Mon Dieu,*" Albert said in disbelief. "How could I be so unlucky?"

What are you thinking of, to have disobeyed your orders so completely? Albert mused. *Now it is clear why you had me locked up. But could you not have put me ashore?*

"Ah, Penfeld," Villeneuve remarked, noticing Albert's presence. "Our emperor wants the pillage of the Mediterranean, and that is what he shall have."

"Pardon me, sir," Albert said, "but our emperor wanted that six weeks ago. Now he has asked you to stand down."

Noticing some of his men had overheard the conversation, Admiral Villeneuve clasped Albert on the shoulder, turning him around and walking him to the stern railing. "Do you see that?" the admiral asked, gesturing grandly around the horizon. "That is the combined fleet of the French and Spanish navies. Second to none in the world."

Albert gazed out into the darkness and saw the ghostly shadows of the warships trailing along behind them. He tried to count them all.

"Thirty-three," Villeneuve said. "The British have moved off-station. Now is the moment for us to run Gibraltar, and then we shall have the entire Mediterranean at our disposal."

"But what of the explicit orders to the contrary?"

"One successful campaign will redeem me in the eyes of the emperor," Villeneuve asserted. "I have not come this far to let my career sink now."

"And what of my return to my company?" Albert questioned, trying to think of any excuse to get ashore and contact Admiral Rossily, or anyone.

"My boy, you will be revered and respected eternally for taking part in this voyage. We are about to change history, and not a man will live who won't wish to have been on the seas with us this day." Seeing the concern still on Albert's face, the admiral spoke more practically. "You will be put off in Marseilles when we reach it, and I will send a letter with you explaining what. . ."

Admiral Villeneuve's words were cut off by a report from the signal lieutenant. "Beg pardon, sir," the young officer said. "Captain's compliments. He desires you to know that the British fleet is in sight."

"What?" Villeneuve exploded.

"*Oui, mon admiral.* It appears they were not off-station, but only over the horizon. They are on course to intercept us in five to six hours."

"Can we make Gibraltar?"

"No, Admiral. If we wear ship now, we may possibly make it back to Cadíz." This was said in such a way as to firmly convey the fact of its impossibility.

"So ordered," Villeneuve replied, quickly losing his nerve and confidence in the invincibility of the combined fleet.

"Young man," he said to Albert, "it is still a great day. If we are brought to battle, then so be it. We will give the emperor even more than he asks, eh?"

"Admiral," Albert said coldly, "since you have carried me into a battle, the least you can do is let me fight."

"But of course."

"But not," Albert continued, "under your command. With your permission, I wish to be assigned a place on another ship."

"Very well," Villeneuve agreed stiffly. "The captain of the *Redoutable* is returning to his vessel. You are to serve aboard her."

The "Nelson touch," as the admiral liked to style it, consisted of doing the unexpected. In the case of Trafalgar he did exactly that. Against almost all strategic thinking of the time, Lord Nelson divided his force into two divisions. Also contrary to naval dictum, he did not intend the two fleets to pass beside each other, exchanging broadsides, but rather aimed his two columns of ships at breaking through the enemy line.

The drawback to this strategy was immediately obvious: the French and Spanish ships were able to bring their guns to bear on the attacking English long before their line had been penetrated.

A heavy shell sailed toward the *Victory*. Just short of striking the deck, it splashed in the water. Another shot was fired. It too fell short, and another. William waited expectantly as the next shell flew straight over the deck, tearing through the topgallant mast and yard. With this ranging fire completed, almost every gun on the French line fired at once. Hundreds of shots raked the decks of the *Victory* at once, smashing heavily into them and causing great havoc, though the command had not yet been given for them to fire.

William stood at his post on the poop deck, waiting for the signal to begin firing. Another storm of cannon-balls showered the *Victory* like black hail. Some seven or eight enemy vessels had singled out the flagship for the attention of their guns.

Casting a glance behind him, William saw the exact moment that a shell sliced into the amiable John Scott, the admiral's secretary.

Automatically William shouted, "Over the side with him, men." As heartless as it seemed, proper working of the ship and its guns could not be interrupted by stumbling over corpses. William and three others left the rail to tumble Scott's remains into the sea.

At the instant they crossed the deck, a twenty-four-pound shot sliced inside the rail, killing eight of William's marines where they stood.

Where I was just standing, William thought as he heaved body after body over the side.

The *Victory* was also firing now, half her one hundred and four guns letting go at once with a roar that deafened and a cloud of smoke that enveloped the ship in an impenetrable curtain. It was so thick that it choked the eyes as well as the nose.

Heavy fire now raked the ship badly from both sides. Only ten feet away from where William stood, impatient for the order to fire his musket, one of the signal flag lockers exploded into splinters and shreds of canvas, striking the signal officer with a jagged wooden beam. William panted as he stared. The deck was awash in blood. Mechanically he grabbed for a sand bucket and sluiced it over the hot gore.

Finally the order came for the riflemen to prepare to fire, and he forgot everything else as he took aim. Selecting a man in officer's dress on the quarterdeck of the *Bucentaure*, William fired. Whipping out ramrod and cartridges, he loaded and fired again and again.

As the *Victory* cut hard aport just aft of the *Bucentaure,* the British warship let go a raking broadside into the windows of the stern gallery. The towering ships-of-the-line were so close that *Victory* ran against a French seventy-four, the *Redoutable.* The rigging of the two ships snarled, and the *Victory*'s starboard smacked hard against the enemy's side, exchanging broadsides with their gunports touching.

Three hundred French marines climbed into the *Redoutable*'s spanker, preparing to board. As the two ships ground against each other the French soldiers leaped across. The shouting caught William's attention, and he led a charge toward the attackers. Foiling the French charge before it was effectively launched, the Royal Marines, armed with muskets and cutlasses, surprised them. William helped Captain Adair train a carronade on the boarding party, and a howl of grapeshot hurtled through the air. With one sweeping close-range blast, the Frenchmen were cleaned off the decks like wind-blown leaves.

The *Victory* slowed to a drift with the two ships still locked in a fatal embrace. Back at his post once more, William took aim at a Frenchman on the *Redoutable*'s quarterdeck who was wearing a sky-blue uniform. Just as William cocked the hammer back and pulled the trigger, a racing powder monkey toting a wooden keg containing a charge of gunpowder sprinted past the man. The ball struck the unlucky boy instead of the intended victim, decorating the blue tunic with a spray of blood.

The victim flung his arms into the air, leaping from the shock of the strike. The man in blue hit the deck as the keg went bouncing. William dived behind cover in case the powder should go off. It rolled toward the gangway and tumbled onto the *Redoutable*'s upper gun deck.

Albert was stunned by the blast of warm blood that flooded over his face. His jaw hung agape as the powder monkey, a mere boy of ten or eleven, collapsed on the deck, letting go of his deadly cargo. Realizing the mus-ketshot had been intended for him, Albert dropped to his knees below the rail. Scrambling for the boy, he began to pull him to safety, then noticed the blank stare of death in his eyes. This one could not be saved.

"Over with him!" an officer shouted. The boy's body lay limp and heavy as Albert heaved him up and over-board. Even in the din of roaring cannonfire, Albert waited for and heard the splash that indicated the boy was gone forever.

Crouching still, Albert wiped the boy's blood from his eyes, wondering if he would live through the day.

The great ship lurched as the helmsman freed her from the tangled rigging of the *Victory*. The French marines regrouped on the portside to fire volley after volley into the *Victory*'s deck. Another cannonblast from the British ship and several soldiers disappeared, along with a section of railing. Their muskets clattered to the deck near Albert, and he reached for one, finding it unfired, still cocked . . . though its owner had been blown to bits.

Bounding to a vantage point hard over the *Victory*'s quarterdeck, Albert allied himself with a group of sol-diers there. Some had climbed aloft to fire down on the enemy deck.

Sighting the musket across the saltwater crevasse, Albert let his aim fall on an officer covered with glittering medals dangling from his chest.

"The fool," Albert said. Slowly tightening his trigger finger and clenching his teeth, Albert heard a shot ring out a split second before he fired, then shots whipped past from above and both sides. Albert looked again to the deck of the *Victory* in time to see the decorated officer fall.

Admiral Nelson's legs gave way. He twisted to the deck, landing facedown in the red sandpile that remained from the death of his secretary three quarters of an hour before. Marine Sergeant-Major Secker rushed over to aid Captain Hardy with his lordship. Hardy rolled Nelson onto his back.

Secker looked frantically around, finally spotting William through the drifting wall of smoke. "Lieutenant Sutton!" he shouted.

William looked up from sighting along the musket barrel, then caught sight of Secker hunched over the admiral. He hurriedly triggered off the shot and laid his weapon down in response to Secker's call.

Arriving beside a knot of huddled figures, William overheard Captain Hardy express hope that the wound would not prove fatal.

Nelson, conscious and looking about though pale and pinched in his features, related that it was what he'd seen in a dream. "They have done for me at last, Hardy," he gasped.

"I trust it is not so," Hardy answered worriedly.

"I tell you it is so. My backbone is shot through."

Captain Hardy grimaced in denial.

"Now steady yourself, Admiral," Sergeant-Major Secker instructed. "Sutton here and I must get you belowdecks." He motioned for William to help lift. William knew that the entire fleet was engaged, yet he could not help wondering if all was lost because of this one casualty.

Captain Hardy pointed aft. "Carry him to the cockpit."

As William and Secker did as he instructed, Admiral Nelson seemingly responded to William's unspoken concerns. The admiral covered his face with a handkerchief, also pulling it over what medals he could. William was astounded by this courageous action of a great leader: hiding himself so as not to discourage those around him. To be in the throes of death and yet to think of the men around you, he concluded, was much greater than an ordinary human's thoughts.

Down into the bowels of the ship they carried the stricken commander. Reaching the decks below the waterline, Hardy began shouting, "Doctor Beatty! Attend at once!"

Surgeon Beatty looked up from examining two officers. They were both already dead. Seeing the handkerchief fall from Nelson's face, Beatty choked back a cry of dismay.

"Oh, dear," Beatty fretted. "Come, we must take him to the midshipmen's berths."

Nelson's eyes weakly rolled open and he said thickly, "Ah, Mr. Beatty! You can do nothing for me. I have but a short time to live. My back is shot through."

William, Captain Hardy, and Secker returned to their duties. The battle continued to rage. Both the *Victory* and the *Redoutable* were in shambles, their decks littered with shattered masts, fallen rigging, and dying men. Hardy dispatched William to examine the damage belowdecks. "And tell the admiral I will return to see him again presently."

On the gun decks all the bulkheads echoed from the cannonfire outside. Because the fighting was so close, and since the danger of fire was so great, the crews adopted a new technique. They loaded three rounds at a time to only one charge of powder. Firemen stood ready with buckets of water, dousing any flaming wadding.

The guns still in action were manned and firing

steadily. No discouragement had penetrated to the fighting men of the *Victory*.

On his way aft, William again passed the dying admiral. Nelson was stripped of his clothes and covered with a sheet. He had grown more delirious with every passing minute. "Doctor," he called in a low whisper, grabbing the doctor's forearm, "I told you so."

Beatty leaned over the bedside close to Nelson.

"Doctor, am I gone?" He attempted to lift his head from the pillow. "I have to leave Lady Hamilton and my daughter, Horatia, as a legacy to my country."

"Yes, yes, your Lordship. I shall see to it."

Then Nelson asked to see Hardy.

Beatty turned to William who had been standing there watching dumbly. "Milord," William said, "Captain Hardy regrets that the demands of the present action do not permit him to attend you just now. He will come as directly as possible."

Almost blinded now, Nelson called out, "Who is that speaking?"

Upon being told William's identity, Nelson remarked, "Good man, Sutton. Remember me to your grandfather."

Then Nelson motioned to him, saying, "Drink, drink. . . ."

William ladled some cool water into his mouth just

as Hardy hurried up. "We are holding very well, your Lordship. We have twelve or fourteen of the enemy's ships in our possession, but five of their leading ships have tacked and show an intention of bearing down upon the *Victory*. I have therefore called two or three of our fresh ships round to us, and have no doubt of giving them a drubbing."

"I hope then, that none of our ships have struck. Have they, Hardy?"

"None, milord," answered Hardy. "There is no fear of that."

William grew restless, as he felt that his presence was somehow becoming a violation of the needed privacy of the two friends. "If there is nothing I can do here, I shall return to deck, so I may rejoin the fight."

Captain Hardy nodded. "Yes, Sutton."

Addressing Admiral Nelson, William said, "With your permission, your Lordship."

"See to your duty, Sutton," he said. "God be praised. I have done mine."

William played these words over and over again in his mind as he ventured to the fighting once more. Men fell on his right and left. William continued loading and firing without regard for his own safety.

A loud crack sounded when a section of spars and mizzen rigging broke and drooped downward over the deck. William glanced up, noticed that its fall was stopped by a tangle of ropes, and went back to reloading.

Standing near the rail, he was halfway through another cycle of loading and firing when the cracking of wood and snapping of ropes sounded again. A chunk of mizzenmast, suspended like a giant pendulum, dropped free from its stays and swung right for William. Without time to think, William dived over the side.

Albert had fired only twice when the mast came down above him. Hearing the violent cracks, he moved to safety a second before. It appeared that all was lost for the *Redoutable*. Her captain had long since signaled for reinforcement ships, yet they were held at bay by the English.

So it was that the *Redoutable* sat lamely in the center of a British ring of fire, catching shot from all directions as the outside of that ring repelled their only hope. Tethered in an embrace of death to the *Victory*, she was also pummeled without mercy by the eighty-nine-gun *Temeraire*.

Wood from the rails, hull, and decks was flitting away constantly as if a master carver intended to remake the warship into a child's toy. *The captain must be dead*, Albert thought. *Why else would they not strike their colors?*

Taking shelter below the stump of the mizzenmast, Albert glanced around the deck, acknowledging the devastation. An oddly complacent comprehension swept through his thoughts, and Albert felt he was going to die. Rising slowly as if lifted by the sulfurous air, he moved to the portside. Vaguely he heard voices call to him, saying, "get down," but as if from a great distance. He was fully conscious of the danger around him but was compelled to look over the side and into the depths below.

As he did so, a break in the looming smoke revealed a French vessel charging between two British ships, coming to aid the *Redoutable*. His premonition of death was shaken, and he was again instilled with the fear of it. He wondered if he might survive after all.

A loud crash and impact just below his feet turned the world upside down. He flew through the air, seemingly getting a view of the entire battle from above. Cold seawater poured sense back into his mind, and all at once he felt the pain of burns on his back, sustained in the explosion. Albert floundered in the icy blackness as the scream of fear filled his ears. He did not want to drown. "Please, God," he pleaded. "For Angelique and the baby."

He had not finished praying, but neither had he drowned, when a large section of the *Redoutable's* heavy decking tapped him gently on the shoulder, as a friend would pat another. He clung to it, thanking God, and watching the continuing action around him. He saw the name of the French vessel that had broken through the ring: it was the *Fougueux*, and she was firing both broadsides at once as she rushed on toward the distressed *Redoutable*. Albert managed a smile as the cannonshots bored into the *Victory*, flinging men into the water in the same manner as befell him.

Instead of landing in the ocean as he expected, William smashed into a drifting longboat that had broken free of being towed astern and floated into the battle. He landed heavily on his head and shoulder. The rebound from the impact flung him then into the water. Before his sight faded to black, William felt a spasm seize his body and tasted metallic blood in his mouth.

Slipping beneath the waves, William flung his arms about blindly, wildly, searching for something to hang on to. His fingers scrabbled at a broken spar, but his arms held no strength with which to cling to life. He dropped into the depths, convinced that his life was ending.

When he felt something grab his wrist and yank him upward, William at first refused to believe it. He thought he was already dead and expected to hear the voice of God. Coughing and gagging on the seawater, his senses slowly came back to him. He felt a hand holding him on to a piece of debris.

As he opened his eyes, he was staring into his own face. The thick dark hair, now soaked with water, green eyes, and angular jaw were mirror images of his own. William blinked and thought again that he was dead. He must be seeing his own features from the other side of the grave.

William looked down at his arm, which the other figure was still tightly squeezing. With surprise in his voice he asked, "I am not dead then?"

The other said nothing, only stared back curiously. William shook the water from his eyes and took the opportunity to study his rescuer. The other man was wearing a light-blue cavalry uniform—French, and stained with blood. William was confused. The man could have been his twin.

The sounds of battle grew faintly distant—and not only because the men were drifting away from the ships. William grew excited. *Could it be*, he wondered, *could it be that my brother is somehow alive?*

There was no other explanation. William realized that by some chance, no, by some act of God, they were brought together in the very act of killing one another.

William exclaimed, "My brother! Charles Sutton! It must be you! You are not dead!"

Albert refused the connection in broken English. "I am Albert Penfeld. Not Charles Sutton."

William tried hard to persuade him. "But how can you deny it? Look at me. We look identical! Listen, when I was a young boy, I was traveling on board the ship *Hermes* with my parents when a terrible storm came along. The ship sank, and my father and twin brother were lost at sea."

"I do not..."

"I am five and twenty years of age," William said abruptly. "How old are you?"

"Also twenty-five," Albert blurted out. "But this is absurd! I am related to no Englishman."

Even as he spoke the words of denial, the expression in his eyes carried the opposite message to William. "Then why did you save me," he demanded, "if we are enemies?"

To this Albert had an answer prepared. "It is not because I know you to be my brother. It is not because I saw you and you look like me, nor was it because I am a traitor. I am recently married, and when I saw you crash down and start to sink, I knew you would surely die unless I helped you."

William was confused. "But why would you save an Englishman? On the decks we would try to kill each other. We are sworn enemies, you and I, Albert. We are like Napoleon and King George on this piece of wood in the water, and yet we do not try to kill each other."

"On your ship, you are English. On my ship, I am French. We are but soda and vinegar. We bubble and hiss at each other until both are dead. But in the water we are only doomed men if one would not save the other. Nothing else. I saved you because I know my Angelique would want me to . . . would hope an Englishman would do for me the same."

William looked around at the huge vessels that had drifted apart from them. Once again his attention returned to battle, though now it seemed that the roar of cannons had stopped. Only the sulfurous aroma of powder remained. A low, thick cloud of smoke drifted up to them. "Then I must thank you, Albert, for saving my life. I owe you my life . . . my brother."

Albert accepted his gratitude, but answered, "You owe me nothing." Then abruptly he added, "Tell me your surname again."

"Sutton," William said urgently. "William Sutton . . . and you are Charles." With this Albert pushed off from the broken shard of longboat and began swimming toward the nearest French vessel.

"Wait!" William called. Albert turned. "You may deny me, but our mother and grandfather . . . still live. If ever we should meet again on the battlefield, I swear not to harm you, but to try and protect you. And if ever we should meet on neutral ground, we shall be the best of friends."

The sound of oars came from behind William. An English voice called out, "Ahoy, there. Are you all right?"

"Fine. I was saved by ..." William looked around for Albert. He listened, hearing a slight splashing in the close fog of gunpowder smoke. At the last moment before it was swallowed up completely, William caught sight of a sky-blue uniform, bearing off toward the French ship.

"What's that you say saved you?"

William did not answer immediately; he was still staring into the fog. As the boat rowed over to him, William realized his life had changed forever. And now, so too had his brother's.

The boatman called out to him again, "I say! Are you all right?"

William whispered the words, "I'm fine now. My God has delivered me and ... my brother!"

HISTORICAL NOTE

Admiral Horatio Nelson, though mortally wounded in the battle of Trafalgar, survived long enough to know his strategy was successful. The combined French and Spanish naval forces were decimated, eliminating the threat of French invasion.

Though Trafalgar was not the end of the war, it saw the end of Napoleon's plans for expansion as he could no longer pose a threat at sea. Ten more years of war followed, marking the gradual decline of France's efforts to dominate Europe.

Destroying the maritime forces of France and Spain left Britain's navy the undisputed ruler of the sea for the next one hundred years. For this reason the battle of Trafalgar has been noted as perhaps the most significant naval battle in the history of the world.